D1315385

THEY DO IT IN CHURCH

THEY DO IT IN CHURCH

TOPSY GREGORY

ABINGDON PRESS
NASHVILLE & NEW YORK

THEY DO IT IN CHURCH

ISBN 0-687-41651-5

Library of Congress Catalog Card Number: 71-160794

SET UP, PRINTED, AND BOUND BY THE
PARTHENON PRESS, AT NASHVILLE,
TENNESSEE, UNITED STATES OF AMERICA

IN MEMORY OF
MY MOTHER

A VERY SERIOUS PERSON
WHOM MY FATHER OFTEN
THOUGHT HILARIOUS

THEY
DO IT IN
CHURCH

1. The sinking sun thrust its hot red light against the Iowa corn, forcing each stalk shadow to lie down like a gaunt old man on an earthen mattress. A person could get lost down there if he didn't stick to the road. Lizzie blotted her sweaty face. Her Saturday bath hadn't lasted half an hour. She felt gummy in the creases already. Most good things don't last. She'd found that out when she was only eight. She'd gone into Dobbin's stall and braided his mane, four braids each side, each intertwined with pretty green rag. Took an hour, what with Dobbin shaking off flies and darned near upsetting the old chair she stood on. And how long did it last?

My Lord, the minute Willie saw it he went cussing to Mother. "That fool kid's got Dobbin looking like a freak. I ain't taking Anita out with no freak horse between the shafts."

"Unbraid it then," Mother said. But his stiff white collar was already showing yellowish where the sweat was soaking in; he wouldn't go near the horse, might get dirty. So Lizzie had to undo all her work.

Twelve years back that was, and it still made her brown eyes smolder and her blackbird-wing eyebrows move closer. "I hate men," she told herself and kicked the blossom off a weed underfoot. She lifted her eyes and saw the distant church rooftop red-gold with sunshine. On the way to confession is no time to be mad. Still, you'd have to be a saint not to hate men sometimes, the smart-alecks. A girl's good enough to gather eggs everyday, blow, snow, or melting August. But let something interesting be happening and see how fast the men would say your place is in the house. She'd never seen a birthing, sow or cow. Men kept you tied to the house and you couldn't even have an opinion about that. Say it needed painting and they'd brush it on the barns instead. Women had no say. Not that she wanted to vote, to take a bath in the middle of the week and go mark "X's" next to names you didn't even know. Only men were crazy about such stuff. She'd never understand 'em. Yet her sister Lil was coaching her to catch one. When Lil was eighteen, she caught Ed Kraemer; easy for her, with her trim shape and her beautiful blonde pompadour. Ed lived down the road apiece with his two brothers, Leo and Cletus. The families had known each other for years. Leo stood up for his brother and Marie was bridesmaid. Nobody was surprised when Leo and Marie got married the next summer. "Lizzie goes next, and Cletus gets her," everybody said.

But Cletus maybe didn't want her. He never asked. Friendly at church, danced couple times at the socials, and last summer he sat with her and Ed and Lil at the strawberry festival. When Cletus took her off for a walk, Lil had winked knowingly at Ed. But nothing came of it. As Lizzie had explained when she got undressed that night (she was living with Lil and Ed since the folks had died), "I could just scream. He's so nice and real polite, but he never says nothing about marriage."

"What did you talk about when you went towards the willows at the creek?"

"Brooder houses."

"Give it time," Lil said to comfort Lizzie. Then thinking how underfoot an unmarried sister can get, Lil added, "You've got to encourage a man. You're here, they're there. You got to get 'em thinking about how nice you'd be together. Work on it."

Lizzie, who had never gone beyond the fourth grade, did not consider herself stupid. I'll just wait my opportunity, she told herself, and opportunity knocked the end of that very June; not the timorous tapping she would have expected from Cletus, but an assured, cocky rapping. It came from the hand of Thomas Davis, fresh from City Commercial College. He'd left his rig under the elm and wondered if he could water his horse. And he wanted to offer condolences. He'd heard about their parents' passing away, but couldn't get away—school, you know.

"He wouldn't have come, just wanted to drag in *school*," Lil thought. She made excuses and got back to her jelly-making.

Lizzie showed Thomas to the pump and the horse trough, then insisted on fetching a fresh cup for

Thomas' use. "Don't bother, I'll use the dipper," he said, but waited for her return with one of Lil's dark blue and white cups from Japan. "That was splendid," he said. "So refreshing this humid day."

Cities and well-groomed people and social amenities in the Land of Could-Be flashed through Lizzie's mind when he spoke so elegantly. She quickly resolved upon a plan. Detain him. Move slow and deliberate, but grab fast if he looked to get away. Maybe while they sat she could think up something to interest him. "Awful hot today. Let's sit awhile. You shouldn't overdo, Thomas." Little did she know it, but with those four words, Lizzie won her man. Nobody had ever said anything so appealing to Thomas before. His father, a farmer, had shocked his sensibilities by inviting him to get off his butt to earn his keep. His mother, who had been a schoolteacher and still read the Bible a lot and taught Sunday school, had defended Thomas and groomed him for higher education. But it depressed him to recall her motives: "He'll never amount to a thing as a farmer, he hasn't got it in him." Thomas was sure he had lots of fine stuff in him. He was also sure it would be a shame to waste it on hard physical work.

And now, here was a girl on *his* side! She would see that he didn't overdo. She cautioned him, "Don't try to see all your old neighbors in one afternoon. Let's sit in the porch swing 'til you cool." They retreated to the porch on the side of the house. Behind the wild cucumber vines they sat, Lizzie pink with Iowa heat and a secret determination, Thomas as cool looking as his clay-colored hair and city-refined hands. He talked on and on, hardly needing the questions she threw out to keep him happily talking about himself. Only once did he become silent. A hummingbird, an iridescent buzz mounted behind a rapier mouth, sought a drink deep within a cucumber blossom. Thomas had never outgrown a childish wonder at God's creation. He and Lizzie watched while the hummingbird sought nectar. In the silence, Thomas reached for her hand and held it. She pulled away, but not too much.

Soon after, he rose to go, but not before Lizzie had promised to go into town with him next Saturday night. It wasn't long before the whole parish knew that Lizzie was Thomas' girl. Visions of living in the city danced in her dreams. No more egg gathering, no more grain to scatter and tin feeders to scour; no more hitching up on Sundays while the men finished early chores; she and Thomas would walk to church in town; that is, if he proposed and she said yes.

He did propose one day during the threshing season. Lil and Lizzie were up to their ears in work, dishes galore stacked at one end of a trestle table and two big dishpans near the middle of the table, one on each side. Their sister Marie and women friends were wiping dishes and bringing up more, and dipping rags in the dishpan to wash off the oilcloths swarming with flies. The men, prickly with chaff and too busy too scratch, had returned to the hot, noisy machine in the yellowed fields.

"Better dump your water, Lizzie, it's awful full of garbage," Lil said.

Lizzie fished a dead fly out of the scummy soap

water and looked for a likely place to dump. Under the elm maybe. As she looked toward the front road, she saw Thomas driving. Funny; he wasn't expected. He had his own business in town, drygoods. He was nattily turned out as usual. (Good for business, he once explained.) "He sure ain't coming to help, I don't suppose, not in them clothes," she said.

"Find out what he wants and get him out of here; I'm a sight," Lil said.

Lizzie took Thomas over to the swing on the shady porch, marveling the while that he could get away on a weekday.

"Oh, I'm my own boss, you know," he said with a smile. "A fellow like me hustles before the holidays, then I can slack off on a hot day like this and come see my girl. Those poor fellows," he waved toward the fields, "are always compelled to be out in the most impossible weather, doing everything to win the gamble against nature." When he saw her puzzled expression, he explained, "I mean, get the hay cut, it's ready whether you are or not; get out of bed rested or not, milking time; thresh even if you die of the heat, grain's ready. Never get done. Now I close shop and that's it."

It sounded like heaven to Lizzie, and she told him how clever he was to have gotten educated and off the farm. Emboldened by her approval, he reached into his vest pocket and brought out a little box. He snapped the lid and there lay a dear little ring of gold. Centered in its prongs was an opal, and around the opal were tiny diamonds. Lizzie's breath pinched in her chest and her pink cheeks bloomed pinker. Was he proposing? Or just showing her some merchandise?

"Like it?"

"It's beautiful." Her voice was a whisper and she lowered the dark fringe of lashes over her eyes. She wouldn't want him or anybody to see how much she wanted that ring.

"Lizzie, what say we get married? Oh, I'm not perfect, but I'd try."

No, he wasn't perfect; she didn't like the way he sat up so close and tight, for one thing. But he'd get over that once they were married. He was just acting like sweethearts were supposed to. Lil and Ed didn't sit close anymore. A little breeze frisked across the cucumber vines. Shadows and sunshine played on the gold band, switched colors on the opal, sparkled the little diamonds. In silence Thomas lifted the ring and slid it on her finger. "Lizzie?"

"Oh yes, Thomas!" He held her too tight and kissed her. She was surprised; she'd expected kisses to be soft things. But she didn't dare think about that—impure thoughts, page 67 *Young Ladies' Companion*, no sin if you try hard to get rid of them.

Thomas did not linger. There was a bit of showman in him and he could just imagine the wild delight of the women when Lizzie waved him down the road and turned back to them to spring her good news. She was getting *him*, and all the ladies present would be sensible of her good fortune. She would live in town and her husband would be one of the local merchants, an usher at church too, and maybe an officer in the Foresters—well, eventually—at twenty-five he was a little young. How the hens would cluck over the beautiful ring! How fast the news would spread! All the men would hear about it when the big girls carried out fresh drinking water to the fields.

It was only two days later that Cletus came back to see Ed about something in the barn. When Lil saw his stricken face, she called him into the kitchen for a lemonade. Lizzie came just then from a back bedroom. She looked like she wanted to run, but Lil asked her to cut the noodles lying ready on the kitchen table, before the dough dried out. "Got to see Ed a minute, be right back." She left the house.

Lizzie took a defensive stance behind the table, left hand over the ribbons of dough, right hand poised above with a sharp butcher knife. She saw the ring on her finger. Not wishing to get flour dust into it, she dropped her knife and began to twist it off.

"So it's true, you are engaged . . . Lizzie, what'd you do that for?" Cletus' sunburned face looked like old leather; there wasn't a trace of his lively copper glow there.

"Why not?" Her black brows flew together and her dark eyes shot sparks.

"I was always gonna marry you."

"Were you?"

"Ed married Lil, and Leo married Marie, didn't he?"

"Yes . . . Well . . . ?"

"I was always gonna marry you."

Lizzie picked up the butcher knife, dug her left fingers into the dough strips, and whacked at the pile.

A dozen noodles curled away from the knife. No good; wide on one end, hairy fine on the other. She adjusted her fingers to the angle she had cut and tried again. It was worse; she felt the knife scrape a tiny bit of nail off her middle finger as it came down. She continued to whack away. She couldn't bear to look up at Cletus. She didn't want to feel bad, and she didn't want to watch if he suffered. She had no idea what to say, what hope to offer him. He left soon and Lizzie's hand steadied as she attacked the noodles at a faster pace. "He could've said something," she seethed while she chopped. "How'd I know he was ever gonna?"

"He could've said something," she cried while she tossed forkfuls of noodles into the air, letting them drop back to dust themselves again and again in the flour.

"Just anything," she mourned as she washed her hands and put on the little gold band with the tiny opal and the diamond chips.

Well, she'd caught her man, Lizzie told herself grimly. She gave a stone a good kick and sent it scudding ahead on the road to church. She'd caught him, plump, rosy-faced Lizzie with the toil-creased hands and the fruit-stained nails. Got him away from the city girls. Two days of being out of her mind with joy, then Cletus had come along and spoiled it all. She caught up with the stone and gave it another kick, but not so hard. Men make more trouble! And now she was on her way to ask old Father Schwartz what she should do.

I wish Mother was alive so I could talk to her, she

thought. Promptly she unwished it. Mother would ask all sorts of questions and her eyes would bore right into mine and maybe she'd twist things so that it'd be my fault that I'm in this pickle. Father Schwartz will be better. He doesn't know me from Adam when he sits behind the wooden grillwork with his ear up against it to listen. It's easier to ask real personal questions in the dark; I could even pretend I was asking for a friend.

She stopped kicking the stone now, too near church. Soon she went up the steps and into the dimming interior. There were only four people there. She'd have to hurry if she was going to prepare properly.

1. Examination of conscience. That wasn't too hard. Same old sins, same old omissions. More omissions than sins.

2. Firm purpose of amendment. That took longer, because it wasn't any good unless you were truly sorry for your sins. "Who will give a font of tears to mine eyes that day and night I may weep for my sins?" Sometimes she tried for as much as twenty minutes before the tears came. No time for that tonight; not enough people ahead of her.

3. Confession to a priest. Wouldn't take too long, she hadn't done much. Mainly she was coming to ask the big question. She could ask Father after Mass tomorrow, but then it wouldn't be in the dark and he'd know who she was and what she was talking about. Better here, after confession.

Now it was her turn, and she stepped into the cubicle and let the drapery fall behind her. Carefully she told her sins (she knew it was a sin to make a bad confession) and listened for her penance.

"Go in peace," said old Father Schwartz when he finished the Latin that made her cleansed again.

"Father?"

"Ya?"

"Father, I have a question."

"Ya?"

"Father, can a girl break her engagement?"

"You're engaged to marry?"

"Yes, Father."

"You got a good reason for breaking off the engagement?"

Lizzie's mind raced. Thomas had never failed to show on date night, he didn't drink, he was active in church . . . "No, Father."

"My daughter, it is a sin to break off an engagement without a good and sufficient reason."

Well, that's that, thought Lizzie. I expected as much, but it didn't hurt to ask. And Cletus looks terrible. He doesn't come around our house anymore. Just a shame. Poor Cletus! but it's his own durned fault. I always meant to marry him—how long was he gonna take before he'd ask? How'd I know if he'd *ever* ask?

"Was there something else?" Father's voice came through the grille.

"Uh . . . no, Father. God bless you, Father." She bolted from the confessional. No sense telling Father that she loved Cletus. Crying over spilled milk. She didn't have a good and sufficient reason; Thomas was a good man, and That was That.

2. February, the month of bitter cold, snowbound roads and Lenten fasts, men underfoot and piglets in a box behind the stove. Every morning the sun rose early to watch Ed bend into the wind on his way to the barn chores. Those done, he hurried back into the house, bringing along a piece of harness that needed fixing, his fingers too numb to work in the shed. Or if the wind blew him back empty-handed, he'd bring out shoes that needed resoling or boots that needed stitches.

"This kitchen can't take any more, Ed," Lil told him one morning. "I've hardly got room to iron."

"Pretty soon the pigs will be off the bottle. They stay behind the stove, anyhow."

"Just the same, I'm going to open the front room. Get a fire started in the Franklin and let's move the sewing machine in there. Marie is coming over and Mr. Swayzer is gonna drop off Emma Hammond with the mail. Three weeks here, then she starts on Miller's Cora. Got enough time. We want it nice—like Thomas says, 'Elegant but not osten-*something*.' Says something for our family; all those town girls and he picks Lizzie."

"Says something for him, too. Knew enough to pick a country girl." Regret tinged Ed's voice, for while Lizzie was slow as an ox, she was steady. He'd miss her, come June. He nudged Lil away from the Singer and began squealing its tinned wheels toward the front parlor. "Lemme. You're in no condition."

"Careful, don't knick the Congoleum edges. Lift it." Lil wished Lizzie was moving the machine, instead of him. Men were hard on things.

"I'll make the fire, I'm dressed warmer," Ed said, so Lil set some bread sponge and got on with dishes before Lizzie came in with Mark.

"Going to help Aunt Lizzie?" She threaded a big needle and handed her nephew a woven basket filled with old buttons. Unasked, she picked up some mending and began a story about a little boy who went to market. Sometimes her needle rested while she got lost in the wonderful smells and sounds of market day, and Mark would urge her on.

"Only three," Lil marveled, "but he listens. Shame she won't be here this fall, especially 'cause she'll be married by then. Could be more help this time." Lizzie was only seventeen when Mark was born, so Lil had instructed everybody to keep her out of the bedroom until it was all over. And Mrs. Unke, the midwife, was as good as her word. She saw to it that neither she nor Doc Schwemmer left anything around unfit for Lizzie's virginal eyes. Time enough when she's married, the woman avowed. Dr. Schwemmer was too busy to waste time arguing the point; he left details to Mrs. Unke and delivered Lil of a fine boy.

Mother and Auntie had hoped for a girl, but they didn't remember their disappointment for long. Now Lil was admiring the shape of Mark's head, his button nose, while she set table. Aunt Lizzie was extravagant in praise of the lumpy string of buttons dangling in his plump little hand. "Beautiful. I'll cut off the needle and tie it on your bedpost before we eat. After your nap, we'll show it to Aunt Marie."

" 'Re coming?"

"Every day for awhile. And Mark is gonna help sew after his nap. Aunt Lizzie's gonna get married and wear a beautiful dress," she said. Mark grinned. He too liked make-believe and dress-up.

"Dinner, everybody." They gathered around the table and set to. Lizzie prayed alone, uncomfortable that Lil had grown careless that way. Probably Ed's fault. She didn't expect any such trouble with Thomas; he was different. Twice she'd eaten at his parents' home and Mr. Davis said grace with a flourish that befitted the husband of a Sunday school teacher. There was an aura about those meals that she'd never sensed at Lil's. Mrs. Davis, or maybe Thomas himself, would make biblical references, and while Lizzie didn't understand a word of it, she felt holy to be in such august company.

"Please pass the bread," Mr. Davis might say.

"Staff of life," his son would comment.

"Man does not live by bread alone, Thomas. Pass Lizzie the jelly." Mrs. Davis won blue ribbons for her currant jelly.

22

Once even Mr. Davis played the game, if game it was. "Behold the lamb," he said as he carved a leg of mutton. Lizzie thought theirs were city manners, no rough give-and-take like most farmers. They were aware of God, and out loud.

It was different here with Lil and Ed. The meal done, Ed bolted and left for the barn. Lil began to scrape dishes and Lizzie got up to put Mark to bed for his nap, but not until she'd said Grace After Meals. She was not one to assert herself, except for religious causes. By the time Mark was disposed of, Marie and Emma Hammond were there and the living room was warm. Emma began by spreading a clean old sheet under and around the Singer. "We'll start with the bridal dress, then if we have to hurry things, it'll be the matron of honor's dress or Mark's breeches," she said, but only to tease. In twenty-six years she had never failed to finish on time. Her method: Do the bridal dress first before they get jittery and turn ugly. Not that Lizzie would give trouble. That girl, with her short waist and broad shoulders, had no illusions about being stylish. "I'm shapely as a potato sack," she commented when Emma was pinning and adjusting pattern pieces. Emma, kind and with an eye toward future business, stoutly denied it.

"Who wants to be all skin and bone? Thomas wouldn't like that, I'm sure."

Lizzie's eyelids shut and a dull flush swept across her cheeks to her ear lobes. Goodness, she's sure skitterish, thought Emma, her mouth full of pins. She'll get over it—they have to when they marry, said the practical

Miss Hammond. "Lil, you can start sewing up the gores. Cut the skirt at home. I'll cut the bodice with Lizzie here."

Marie fingered the bombazine spread on the table. It was the color of tea with a bit of milk poured in, shimmering where it lay over the scissors and pincushion. "It's beautiful."

"Gorgeous, the way it drapes," Emma agreed.

"Don't you think it's too hot for June?" Lil asked.

"I ain't goona be cool, no matter what," said Lizzie. "Got to be something fancier than just cotton. Besides, bombazine don't wilt. I sweat like a horse in summer."

All afternoon the ladies bustled from kitchen table to sewing machine and ironing board, running to and from the range where one flatiron heated while they used the other. The treadle on the sewing machine seldom quit its rocking; if Emma's foot wasn't on it, Marie's or Lil's was. Now Lil was steaming open a skirt seam and Marie was at the stove holding a flatiron near her cheek to test it. "Remember the day you came running in the house all excited because 'two dogs were stuck together' and couldn't get apart?" she asked her sister.

"I was younger then." Marie's lips thinned into a straight line of displeasure.

"Not that young," Lil persisted. "We were in this very room and you were wearing your engagement ring, that's how young you were." She chuckled.

Lizzie looked up from her basting. She'd never heard this one. Apparently the story was finished. What was the point? Lil sponged another seam while Marie turned fiery red. " 'Sfunny," thought Lizzie. Miss Hammond smiled. The shop talk was a fringe benefit that she took home to relive over duller jobs. When Lil left the room, Marie began a story about her and Ed, talking fast and low; Lil would have fits if she overheard. Lizzie trembled between hearing and shutting out Marie's voice. It was her business to listen; she'd soon be married. And it was her duty not to listen; her mother, rest in peace, was firm when Lizzie asked once. "You learn that stuff when you're married, not before."

Ed came into the house. "I'll change the litter. You don't want to mix with that when you're on silk stuff." He headed for the seven motherless piglets behind the stove. I'll like 'em better when they ain't so newborn, Lizzie thought. They look indecent, so pink and naked. She thrust fresh thread into her needle.

"How's it coming? You gonna be all ready second Saturday of June?" Ed was gathering up the last clump of soiled straw.

"I'll be ready," said Lizzie. Emma Hammond was dependable, the dress would get done. And her hope chest was filled. I been getting ready a long time, way before I met Thomas. I want everything nice and clean when I start out. She could see it all now: the house in town with geranium boxes on the porch rail and lilacs in the backyard. And the fences between backyards. Won't it be funny seeing other ladies in their yards hanging out? Would they watch you, see what you wear, how you live? Gee! Well, I'll hang out early and get it in early. They don't have to see everything. Sudden shock: Thomas would be coming home noons, his shop was only three blocks away. What when it's rainy and things don't dry good? She smiled. I'll hang my underwear on the inside line and put the sheets and towels on the outsides. Maybe she'd only gone through fourth grade, but like Mother'd always said, she had horse sense. Then another problem arose. Would the chimes at St. Robert's in the city keep her awake? I'm gonna like it when they strike noon and six. We'll say our Angelus together at suppertime. She imagined herself and Thomas in sepia tones, heads bowed, out in a field. There was a scythe at her feet—or was it his?— and a bit of dust on the picture frame. It hung a bit crooked. She forgot that Thomas' field of endeavor was in a store for men and that a scythe would have given him blisters. My own house to clean before lunch, gardening and sewing afternoons, a big hot dinner ready for Thomas at night.

Imagine, dinner at night! That's how he wants it. I expect lots of things are gonna be different, marrying a man from the city. While he reads the paper—he's a great reader—I'll get the dishes done, then we can walk together on the wooden sidewalks, won't that be fun? And by bedtime we'll be so tired we'll go right to sleep. I'll never hear St. Robert's gongs. Her head snapped and she straightened up suddenly. She wouldn't be ready in June if she fell asleep at her sewing. With fresh determination she picked up her needle.

3. Thomas reached up to the third shelf and took down the big gray book with its maroon leather-trimmed corners and gilt lettering, "Ledger." He shoved aside the ties and shirts which he had recently shown a customer and hadn't put away. He walked over to the till and counted the money in the drawer again. Then he unscrewed the cap from his fountain pen, walked back to his ledger and opened it on page one. A few entries were debts: rent, two dozen collars, salary to the boy who washed the window—it was only a dime, but Thomas meant to keep meticulous records and always balance out.

Three times as many entries were in the column marked "Credits." He smiled with satisfaction. If he realized that the debts were mostly large amounts and the credits were quite small, it did not depress him. He was an incurable optimist—how could a good Christian be otherwise?—and business would build up. How could he lose? The same God that gave Iowa farmers black loam, fat yellow ears of corn, enormous pigs, and creamy milk would give him customers. Just give it time.

As if God were saying "Amen" to Thomas' vote of confidence, a customer came quietly in. There was no tinkle of bells above the door. Thomas had no intention of hamstringing himself with old conventions. His would be a modern store, filling with creative innovations as they would occur to him. And he was sure they would. He'd always been one to look around and say, "Is there a better way?" Even as a little boy, he had experimented with the old order. He was only eight when his mother sent him out to weed the onion patch in her kitchen garden. Thomas didn't even carry along the hoe—why bother? It was heavy and he couldn't use it close to the onions anyhow, only on the outer edges of the rows. Weeds and onion shoots didn't weigh anything hardly, why make hard work of it? So he uprooted all the greens, weeds and onions alike. He planted back each tender shoot of green with a white bulb and tender hairy roots attached.

His father was all for taking young Thomas out to the woodshed when the young onions turned to sodden tan ribbons, but his mother . . .

"Are you still open?" The customer drummed his fingernails on the glass display case and Thomas looked up from his ledger.

"Just closing up, but what can I do for you? Let me show you these fine broadcloth shirts before I put them away."

"No, not today. I just want to leave these collars for the cleaner." He laid four stiff and dirty circles on the counter. "When can I pick them up?"

"The laundry will have them back on Tuesday,"

Thomas replied. I'll have several of the worsteds and twills out on the counter right next to the style book, Thomas told himself as he asked for the customer's name and gave him a claim check. Bet he's the new accountant they got at Four Square Packing Plant. Glad I had my ledger out, we have something in common. "I'm Thomas Davis, been here six months now. Have I met you?"

"No, we just moved here the first. Name's Art Bushke." The men shook hands, Art pleased but surprised at Thomas' enthusiasm.

Thomas began a cordial dissertation on the town's assets, its favorable location, its salubrious weather.

"We could use some rain," Art broke in, and hurried for the door. Some talker, he told himself.

"I'll be looking for you on Tuesday," said Thomas. Now some fellows would say don't waste time on such a customer, he's small potatoes—four collars. But I have vision. He's a white-collar worker, he'll need nice clothes right along. If he's got sons, they'll need clothes. Or maybe he'll get sons. But maybe he'll have all girls. He smiled happily at Mr. Art Bushke's fate. Thomas liked girls, and to heck with making money.

He did not put away the shirts and ties; it could wait for morning. From below the till he brought out a neatly lettered sign, "Will be back at 8:00 A.M. to serve you," and set it in the window against a visored cap. He had printed the sign himself and thought it vastly superior to the customary sign painted on a window shade: "Closed." *Closed* said, "Go away," whereas his sign invited trade. He was a great believer in positive thinking, and he was to say, "My glass is half-full, my wife's is half-empty," but that was to come many years later.

Now he took one last look at his ledger and it occurred to him that it might be a good idea to save the four bottom lines of each page for personal notations and promotional ideas. Having no promotional brainstorms at the moment and being suddenly bored with the necessity of making a living anyhow, he wrote across the bottom lines of the ledger page: "God's in his heaven, All's right with the world. Practice tonight. Pick up Miss Germaine. Ed brings Lizzie." His heart quickened as he thought of Lizzie, her honest ways, her piercing black eyes softened by the pink that rose so easily to her cheeks, her firm roundness, her dear shortness—she came up only to his shoulder. He hoped the sons that they would have would be as tall as he was. It wouldn't matter how short his daughters would be, just so he'd have daughters too. He was very fond of little girls; for a fact, he was fond of most women. If it hadn't been Lizzie, there would have been some other woman, never fear. The romantic twaddle ladies read (he'd seen samples of it in the newspaper serials) was just that— twaddle. Any fellow of intelligence would pick a girl that would grow into a healthy woman and make a good mother for his children. He had no doubts about Lizzie's capabilities; she came from healthy stock and was a great favorite with small children.

He blotted his entry and closed the ledger. I'll put it away tomorrow, he said. He walked to the back of the store, where there was a tiny washroom with a mirror set above the chipped soapstone sink. His bushy hair with its side part and high wave made his face seem even longer. He had a long upper lip upon which he had begun to cultivate a moustache. The new growth, tinged with a carroty red, did not match his other hair at all. He sometimes thought he detected gray in his twenty-five-year-old locks, but it was hard to be sure with hair such an indeterminate color. Not that it mattered too much, he assured himself. It's what's under the scalp that counts. With that he was well content. He washed his hands and cleaned his fingernails. Then wetting a comb, he ran it through his hair. He carefully brushed his shoulders and set the coat seams aright. He walked to the front of the store while groping for a key in his pants pockets. He carried only two, one for the store and one for the cottage that he and Lizzie would move into Saturday. He had rented it without showing it first to her. Women fuss so about such things. He'd simply walked from his rooming house to Hiller & Son's one day and asked Mr. Hiller what was available. He selected a small cottage that was only three blocks away from the shop, paid a month's rent, and pocketed the key. If the house needed attention, let Mr. Hiller worry. Or Lizzie. Women always fussed and fixed. He hummed a tuneless hit and turned the key to lock up for the night.

Now for one of his last meals in a rooming house, and to pick up a rig at Glancey's, pick up the organist, and to church for rehearsal. Ha! Was it possible the ladies didn't know every move, every word? Just another example of female fussing that he'd have to go along with. For himself, he was as ready for marriage as he'd ever be.

Nevertheless, he grew edgy, and because the meal wasn't quite ready, he left and hurried to the stable.

"I'll have her hitched in a wink," old Mike said. "So you're going to join the ranks and give up your freedom."

"I'm getting married, not selling my soul."

"Hump! It ain't the same?" He handed over the reins.

The mare was fresh and the buggy wheels hardly stopped when they got to Miss Germaine's. She was stationed at the big maple marking her lane. Thomas helped her arrange her skirts and portfolios. Then a cluck to the horse, an animated conversation with Miss Germaine (she mostly listened), and soon they arrived at the church.

Lil and Ed were resting on the lowest step and Gracie Harmeyer, who was going to be flower girl, was coaxing them to play Where Does the Baker Live, Up or Down. Lizzie was pacing up and down the dirt walk. She hurried forward. "Miss Germaine, you go right in and arrange your music. Father's waiting. Hello, Thomas." Her flushed cheeks turned even pinker as he kissed her right in front of Lil and everybody. They moved toward the church vestibule and were greeted by Father Schwartz.

"Wasn't too long ago; still remember your cues, Lil? Just remember, Ed, this time you give the bride away, you don't claim her," Father teased. "Come on, everybody, take places."

"I'll chord first and nod *when*," Miss Germaine promised. She arched her fingers, arranged her hips, and began to pump and play the same processional that had carried Lil toward Ed and, a year later, Marie toward Leo. And now Lizzie was to march down the aisle to be claimed by Cletus—Miss Germaine hit b flat instead of b natural just then and quickly corrected herself—Lizzie was to be claimed by Thomas. With half a mind on her music, she beat out the wedding march. The rest of her mind, like a metronome, swung to and fro: THOMasCLEtus THOMasCLEtus THOMasCLEtus. Everybody expected Lizzie to marry Cletus eventually. What happened? 'Spose Thomas swept her off her feet, she decided.

"Miss Germaine, shouldn't Lizzie be almost to the altar by now?"

"What? Oh yes, Lil. Sorry. I forgot to nod." Miss Germaine began the tune again. "Mind your music," she scolded herself severely. "Whatever it was, it's between God and Lizzie." By which she meant to nudge God into taking extra precautions with this marriage. She was a great believer in sticking to your own kind. Thomas with his higher education did not qualify as one of the fold. She rested her hands in her lap. No music during the speaking.

"Who gives this bride in marriage?" Father Schwartz didn't need the practice, having asked at least five hundred couples. Ed stepped forward. Queer—not the giving away, but giving her to Thomas. Hadn't Cletus ever asked her? Had she refused? Well, I ain't the only one puzzled, Ed assured himself; Cletus himself looks

33

like he's been hit on the head with a plank ever since Lizzie began to wear her engagement ring.

"Now," Father Schwartz was saying, "we're going to practice the wedding vows. You answer loud and clear—you know how. Thomas Davis, will you take Lizzie Pierot here present for your lawful wife according to the rite of our holy Mother, the Church?"

"I do."

"Not *quite* so loud," said Father.

"Lizzie Pierot, will you take Thomas Davis here present for your lawful husband according to the rite of our holy Mother, the Church?"

Lizzie bit down on her full red lips. Confusion panicked her for a moment. Mother Church was marrying her to Thomas. Her own mother had hinted about Cletus when Lil and Ed had become engaged. But she was only fifteen then, her mother had died, and Cletus had never proposed. Lizzie bowed to an invisible yoke. Oxlike, she turned from Father Schwartz to Thomas. He smiled.

"You're supposed to say, 'I do,' Lizzie."

Very gravely Lizzie answered, "I do."

"Now join your right hands and say after me: 'I, Thomas Davis—you say Lizzie Pierot when it's your turn—take—say each other's names . . .'" Father Schwartz halted and looked with sympathy down at Lizzie. "It's only practice," he said, for she was breathing heavily and her face was dampening.

But Lizzie didn't look upon wedding practice as a thing to be lightly regarded; it was probably even more binding than getting engaged.

The practice continued for another forty minutes. When Miss Germaine and Lil were satisfied—for it is always the ladies who fuss the most—Ed and Thomas were told that they had done very well indeed. Father Schwartz retired to his rectory and Lil and Ed climbed into their buggy with Gracie. "Mustn't let our little flower girl wilt before Saturday," said Lil.

"Well, thanks for everything," Lizzie said, addressing no one in particular.

"See you Saturday." Thomas dismissed Lil and Ed. "Lizzie, we'll drop off Miss Germaine, than take a ride, shall we?"

"Oh, no you don't," said Lil. "She's coming home with us now. We aren't going to let her get all tired out before the wedding. Come over tomorrow for supper if you like." Thomas had time for only a handclasp, then Lizzie was whisked into the wagon and borne away.

The next two days were always blurs in Lizzie's memory. She played with Mark, ate, dusted furniture, entertained company, said prayers, but in what order or how often she could never remember. There was a meal that Thomas came to—was it supper Friday night?—and they rode about afterward behind Glancey's Dolly, a horse with a leisurely disposition. It was a beautiful night that nothing could mar. When Thomas said, "This is our last night together, *apart* I mean," Lizzie laughed.

"It's all right."

Thomas continued, "Our last night and I want to ask you something. Is there anything about me that you don't like? Because if there is, we don't have to get married, you know."

Lizzie laughed again. She thought she knew what he meant: "Is there something I should reform about me? Because you shouldn't have to put up with it."

He took her laugh to mean 100 percent admiration of his sterling qualities. He kissed her. She took the kiss to mean that he would do everything to change from a sorta stuck-on-me bachelor to a perfect husband.

And so, among candles, flowers, rice, and delusions they were married the next morning.

4. Miss Germaine lifted her wrists after the last chord and dropped her hands into her lap. Then, leaving her sheet music on the rack, she hurried outside to join in congratulating the bridal pair. Greetings and cascades of rice rained down on them, and when Thomas threw back his head to laugh, a sharp pellet hit his open mouth. Startled, he shut it and looked down to see how Lizzie fared. The flat braid above her black pompadour was peppered with grains. He drew his little bride close to him and shielded her head with one extended hand. "Let's run for it, Lizzie," he said.

Among the dozen or so buggies and wagons in the churchyard stood one hired cab, a gilded lily among the country flowers. Ribbons and bows were fastened to lamps, door handles, everywhere, including the shafts. The horse between them looked polished, and satin pompoms were tucked behind his blinders. He wore a wide collar of crepe paper flowers, and between his ears was a concoction of net and artificial lilies of the valley that some wag meant for a bride's veil. "Somebody's sure been busy," Thomas remarked.

"He must've missed the whole Mass," Lizzie said.

Thomas handed her up, then climbed into the driver's seat. He clucked once and when the horse started off, he let the reins go slack. He reached over for Lizzie's small brown hand and brought it to his lips, then set it upon his thigh. There he held it, pressing it under his hand, liking the feel of it against his body. "Lizzie, you're sitting next to the happiest man in the world right now."

"I'm glad."

"That you're sitting next to me?"

"That you're happy."

"Aren't you glad you're next to me?"

"Sort of." She was, but she was not one to tempt the fates. If she was happy that was her own affair, best kept to herself. Say it out loud and spoil it; like it said in the mission magazine she once read, all the Chinamen pretended their babies were girls, then the gods didn't get jealous of their happiness. Good idea.

The horse clopped along while Thomas with no Oriental inhibitions sang his wedding canticle. "Isn't this a gorgeous day? Look at that blue sky. Only God could paint such a blue. The daisies—aren't they dandies? All starchy stiff, like dress shirts with golden circles for cuff links. Hop toad, look out! Stay there under the plantain 'til our coach passes. Ever notice, Lizzie, how graceful plantain is? First the stiff stem full of ribs, then the ribs fanning out through each leaf, all so tough and shiny, then the stiff spears with their green crumbs so soft. Do fairies make coffee with 'em when the crumbs turn hard and brown? I know little girls do."

She was amused. "I shouldn't say it, Thomas, but I think dandelions are pretty when they're in bloom, do you?"

"They are. Why shouldn't you say it?"

"They're weeds, Thomas."

"So they are. Still pretty."

"But you don't encourage weeds, Thomas."

"I admire anything that flowers. I admire clover, dandelions, the tiny blossoms on creeping jenny. . ."

"Not those weeds!"

"Sure, maybe 'cause they *are* weeds. I admire things that keep growing in spite of resistance. Shows spirit."

She did not argue the point. But there's no creeping jenny going to stay in my lawn, she promised herself. She fell silent while Thomas chattered on. When it occurred to her that five rigs had already passed them, she persuaded him to stop talking so much and get up some speed. He released her hand then and told the horse to giddap. Pompoms and streamers bobbled, and soon they turned in at Kraemer's farmhouse.

Lil ushered Lizzie into Mark's bedroom. "Get rid of your rice," she said and opened the hooks and eyes marching down the bride's back. "Lean over the bed. Shake your head."

"Enough to make pudding," Lizzie observed when she saw the grains thick on the bedspread.

"Now, out your bodice." Lil proceeded to check Lizzie backside, modestly leaving any rice up front for the bride to extricate. "Got it all? Gets sharper by the hour."

Lizzie nodded. "Glad you thought of that." She

wanted to say a lot more, for Lil had been mother to her for five years and this was a parting.

Lil placed the last little hook into the last little metal eye and shoved her kid sister out of the bedroom. They went hand in hand across the lawn toward clusters of guests. A shout went up. "Here comes the bride!"

"Hooray! We can start to eat now," said Gracie Harmeyer, and, "Mind your manners, Gracie," her mother said, not meaning a word of it; nobody liked standing around doing nothing. Eating would really start the party.

Lizzie cut the cake, that glorious three-tiered creation Marie had fashioned, using a large washbasin for the bottom layer, a huge iron skillet for the middle layer of batter, and a two-pound butter crock for the baking of the top tier. Last thing yesterday, Marie had put on a thin icing to prime all three layers. Today she'd gotten up shortly after dawn to hurry chores before she decorated her younger sister's wedding cake. "It's too beautiful to eat," Lizzie said, and Marie felt well paid.

Frosty pitchers of fruit punch and tall coffee pots were set on the big tables under the trees. The refreshments were light since everyone who could arrange for someone to do his chores was expected to stay on for the big dinner at two o'clock.

All the Pierot girls felt gratified when thirty people sat down to their dinner. It had taken some borrowing of china and silver and a lot of planning to prepare for both a meal and a wedding. They had washed each other's hair, and Marie, slicing lemons for punch, had capped Lizzie's elbows with lemon rinds and dipped her nails in juice. They sorted jobs to be done first and those that had to be done last, leaving for Lizzie only the tasks that didn't break nails, stain hands, or dirty her shining black pompadour. Their care and planning had paid off. The table was amply set and the bride was pretty as a Dresden figurine with creamy gown, pink cheeks, and a pile of hair shiny as black enamel.

"Ought to be out in the fields, but shucks," said an old neighbor, "some of us gotta show, take her parents' place, sort of." Father Schwartz and Mr. Swayzer nodded agreement.

Miss Hammond said to Miss Germaine, "You sure played a beautiful piece at the offertory. Chills went up and down my spine, honest!"

"Well, I just feel inspired when the bride is so sweet and so grand looking all at once. That dress! I don't know how you do it!"

At the other end of the table, little Mark had been trying to get attention. Now he knelt up on his chair and whispered something in his father's ear. Ed excused himself and took Mark toward the outhouse. When they returned, Lil quietly asked Mark something which no one else heard since so much chattering was going on. For no particular reason, there came a sudden lull in the general conversation just as Mark answered, "No, but Daddy did. Real hard."

Poor Ed blushed beet red. Mr. Davis threw back his head and laughed until his face turned red too. Lil sat very erect and looked stern. Mark ducked his head in confusion and was about to slip off his chair and slide under the table when Thomas came up to him. "Done eating, Mark? Let's get Aunt Lizzie and go see Star." The three of them headed toward the orchard fence where Mark's pony was tied up. Mark broke into a run, glad to be away from the grown-ups.

"Why'd you want to see Star?" Lizzie asked Thomas.

"Didn't especially. But Mark thought people were laughing at him and that can be pretty cruel."

When they returned to the tables, the guests were beginning to leave and Thomas sauntered to where the men were beginning to hitch up.

"Got yourself a nice filly there," said one, pointing toward Lizzie.

"Just don't pull on the bit too hard."

". . . or too soon."

"Give her her head."

"May's well; they don't none of 'em like the harness."

"Sophie does. She'd be lost without a firm grip and a flick of leather on her rump." The men roared with laughter at that one. Sophie was one of the workingest women in the whole parish. Between stints of housework, cooking, washing, soap-making, sewing, and child-bearing, she found time to keep Alfred on his feet and running the farm somewhat.

"Try double harness, Alfred. Maybe Sophie's pulling too big a load."

"Wouldn't work. That Sophie, she's a regular Percheron. Alfred, he's more a . . ." The speaker groped for the right word.

"Shetland?" The wag was gratified at the laugh that went up, but Alfred didn't think it quite fair; it was

Thomas they were supposed to be kidding, so he protested.

"You think Thomas and Lizzie are a matched pair?"

Thomas did not want Lizzie discussed coarsely. He did not think of her as a horse and he wanted to get the conversation on a higher plane. They'd solve their problems in mutual love, having meant it when they promised God " 'til death do us part." Shucks, it couldn't be too hard, not where love abides, Aloud he quoted, "For my yoke is sweet and my burden light."

The wag was delighted with the observation. He set his straw hat between his horse's ears, kissed her long nose, and said, "Pull, Lizzie, for my yoke is sweet and my burden light."

"That's oxes wears yokes," a friend corrected him.

"You calling Lizzie an ox? That sweet little girl?" the wag asked.

Thomas' eyes blazed and he chewed the edge of his moustache for a moment. Then remembering how coarse and uneducated these men were, his anger died. They meant no harm, only amusing themselves. He turned away and walked toward the house.

"I laugh at *his* jokes," the wag complained. "Even if I don't know the point of 'em."

The bride and groom were finally alone. They had lingered on at Lil and Ed's long after the last guests departed. Then, when the sun finally sank behind the flat land, they started for town and their own cottage. Thomas was all for giving the horse free rein, but Lizzie was too excited to permit a slow gait and frequent stops while the horse nibbled grass. "Hurry him up, Thomas," she urged.

"Ah, Lizzie, we've got 'til death do us part. Why hurry now?"

"I don't want to die in this tight dress. I want to die in my nightgown," she said. Her hand flew to her mouth in dismay. What a way to talk!

Thomas' blue eyes twinkled. "I'm sure you're very pretty in your nightgown. I can hardly wait to see your black hair tumbled down, brushed over your shoulders. Giddap, sir. My Lizzie wishes to get out of her corsets," he told the horse, and flicked him lightly.

"Thomas!" Her mouth straightened and her eyebrows winged downward.

"Yes?"

She became tongue-tied. She wanted to explain that she didn't want such talk, not when you could still see out. She wanted to tell him that Ed never talked that way to Lil. Something stopped her; she could just imagine Thomas' reply, *That's because the Kraemers have no imagination.* She remembered he'd said that before, and wondered why it was important anyhow. Ed was steady, his brothers Leo and Cletus, too, and that's what matters. She changed the subject. "I'll bet it's hot in our house, all closed up."

"It's not closed. I left the windows open last time I was there."

"Oh Thomas, what if it had rained?"

"It didn't."

"But if it had?"

"It probably would have run straight down and the

house would have cooled off and nothing got hurt. What's a little water?"

"Oh Thomas, you've got to keep some windows closed when it rains. Some might blow in. You've got to be there and see which side it blows in." She became quite agitated. "Can't you get a move on that horse?" She wanted to get to the poor little cottage before it was completely ruined.

"Giddap!" This time he said it with conviction and the horse knew he meant it. He quickened his gait and Lizzie moved close against Thomas to steady herself. She only half listened to his plans and schemes for improving business but roused quickly when he said, "Well, here we are."

He helped her dismount and led her up the wooden walk and onto the front porch. He pushed open the door, lit a match, and put it to the wick of the fat round kerosene lamp on the living room table. He adjusted the flame and Lizzie replaced the glass chimney. Her black eyes glowed and the lamplight warmed the roses in her cheeks. She looked about and sighed with happiness.

"Want to sit out on the porch while I take the rig to the stable?" Thomas asked.

"Oh, I'd feel funny sitting out there alone. I'll wait for you right here," and she sat down on the mission rocker covered with slick black leatherette. Her toes barely touched the floor.

Thomas brushed his lips to the top of her hair and patted her hand. "Be back in less than ten minutes."

A good time to say my night prayers, Lizzie told

herself. She had a rigid set of prayers and she began on them dutifully. But she was too distracted to get very far. The lamplight threw unfamiliar patterns on the walls. The street sounds distracted her, too. She heard the clop, clop of a horse and somebody roller-skating on a wooden porch. A door banged somewhere and she heard a couple giggling—it sounded right out front. She tried to get on with her prayers and ignore the noises. But she felt all shaken up inside, deserted in a foreign land. "He'll soon be back," she told herself, and felt worse.

She abandoned her formal prayers. "Dear God," she whispered, "I'm all done living in the country. And now I'm on my own. If I do wrong, it's my own fault now. No more asking Lil. Keep Thomas good and make him holy. I wouldn't want him on my conscience. And when we have kids, make 'em good and keep 'em that way; I wouldn't want to be responsible. I'll feed 'em and dress 'em and love 'em, but You gotta keep 'em good. I dunno. I had it good at Lil's. Maybe I should have just stayed there and helped her raise her family."

This is not getting my prayers said, she told herself. She began again where she had sidetracked. "Remember, O most blessed Virgin, Mary, that never was it known . . ." She heard quick footsteps on the walk, and then Thomas was letting himself in at the door.

"Hello, ma'am, is your husband home?" He kissed her quickly, then drew her out of her chair. "Ah, Mrs. Davis. I have you alone at last. Are you tired, Lizzie?"

"Well, it's been a long day, but it sure went fast, didn't it?"

Something in her eyes reminded him of the little lost kids behind the snow fence at County Fair every fall, and he said, "Why don't you go and undress? I'll be in after a few minutes."

"Can you help me with my hooks and eyes?" She hated to ask.

"A pleasure." He gave her his arm and piloted her to the bedroom. One by one he opened the tiny clasps marching down the wedding dress. At the sixth one, he bent down to kiss her soft flesh.

"You cut that out, or I'll . . ."

"You'll what? Go next door and ask Mr. Martin to unhook you?" He saw a blush spread down her neck. Immediately contrite, he spun her around to face him. "Oh, Lizzie, I'm sorry, I shouldn't tease; but I love you so." He finished unhooking the dress, then quietly left for the parlor. He patted the rocker where she had sat, tried the sofa for size, and sprang up again to adjust the lamp mantle. He read a few titles in the glass-fronted bookcase: *Black Beauty, Up from Slavery, The Salesman's Manual, Lives of the Saints.* Without realizing it, he began to pace around the table, hands locked in back, chewing on his sandy moustache.

When he calculated that Lizzie had spent time enough to remove several layers of clothing, he knocked at the bedroom door. "OK?" and when he got no reply he entered. Sitting down on the edge of the bed, he began to unlace his shoes. Lizzie modestly rolled over and faced the wall. He removed his clothes, hanging them carefully in the closet. Timidly he climbed into bed and waited for Lizzie to roll toward him. She didn't stir.

"Lizzie?"

"Huh?"

"Aren't you going to come over this way? Come on now."

She moved backwards toward Thomas' half of the bed and he reached toward her. She got the shock of her life: he was naked, pure mother-naked. Involuntarily she shrank away a bit and Thomas shifted toward her, speaking love and reassurance. She squeezed her eyes tight shut, rolled over, and yielded her body.

5. All that summer, Thomas' bride was pulled in two directions. She greeted every morning with enthusiasm for the housekeeping chores. She dreaded every evening with all the work done except to slip between the muslin sheets on the double bed.

Up softly now. Let him sleep. The moon paled in the west and the mourning doves were beginning to stir in the poplar outside the window. She carried her clothes to the bathroom to dress, then started the fire in the black iron stove in the summer kitchen. She wrested the wash boiler just so over the flame. Thomas always filled it the night before and placed it on the stove, leaving one round iron lid ajar so that she had only to strike a match to the kindling to begin laundry day. She had protested his carrying all those buckets of water the night before. "It's still Sunday," she said. But he said that only servile work was forbidden on the Sabbath, and helping Lizzie was pure pleasure and no more sin than a family picnic.

"And not so much work, if you want to think about it," he added. To Lizzie it sounded so good that it must be wrong, but she submitted to his line of reasoning. After all, she had promised to love, honor, and obey— and it did save a lot of time on Monday.

She blew out the match, watched it blacken and curl into a crooked hook while she thought about Thomas. What kind of religion was his? Seems like he bends the rules to suit himself. Like this wash water: said he didn't mind doing it, therefore it couldn't be servile work. But the way she saw it, did God mind it? and to heck with what Thomas says. Half the time he couldn't prove what he said. Like the time he said he didn't expect there were very many people in hell; there wouldn't have been much point in God creating man if the bulk of them weren't going to be happy with Him in heaven. At first, she went pale at such presumptuous nonsense. When she got her voice, she pointed out that such talk was a sin against one of the three what-cha-callems.

"The what?"

"The three you-knows: faith, hope, charity."

"Theological virtues? Which one? I've got faith, I believe in God. And I certainly hope in Him. And I believe He loves us so much that we will end up in heaven with Him. Where's the sin?"

"Pre . . . pre—presumption. That's it! Practically telling God what He's supposed to do with sinful man. You know darned well, there's plenty people right here in Iowa don't deserve eternal happiness. Well, Iowa's only one state. Add the others, and other countries, other side of the world. There's plenty. There'll be more. The world ain't getting any holier." It was a long speech for Lizzie, and her eyes snapped and her face grew pink with earnestness. Thomas' eyes twinkled and he drew her to himself and kissed her mouth. "Your Napoleon-loving daddy was a Jansenist, but you'll get over it, living with me."

She drew back offended. She hadn't the faintest notion what a Jansenist was. "Don't talk against the dead." And Thomas didn't say another word. But she could tell the way his moustache stretched, he was laughing inside. We'll see, she said inwardly. She couldn't imagine a heaven full of smart-alecks.

Last Monday, taking down wash, she told Mrs. Martin about his strange talk. "You can't change a man, don't even try to," said her neighbor lady, who had been married ten years and knew all about men. Lizzie knew the tactful thing was to nod her head in agreement, but she would never lie, not even by implication, so she just settled her mouth firmly over unspoken words. He'll change, she promised herself. Or else . . .

He sure wasn't changing very fast, she told herself as she put a pot of coffee to boil. She sliced four pieces of bacon and cut off the rind. Then she put them in a skillet and lit a very small fire under it. She brought out currant jelly, the last she and Lil had put up together at Kraemer's. Its color was still good. She sliced three pieces of bread, two for her and one for Thomas. He really didn't eat much for a man. He said he wasn't a farmer and shouldn't eat like one. She wondered privately if it wasn't just a way of showing off, and a peculiar one for a man. She went down cellar for two eggs—it was the coolest place to keep them—and set them near the stove. There was no sound from the

bedroom, so she set the skillet aside and hurried outside to string up her washline.

When she returned, Thomas was shaving. "Morning,
dear. Why so early?" and he laughed. His bride of three
months had managed four different times to get her
wash out on the lines before any other woman in the
block. They hated her for it, but admired the gumption
she showed in accomplishing the feat. "Martin's rooster
is complaining that he can't get his sleep with you
rattling around so early."

Lizzie dimpled with pleasure. "Ready for me to fry
'em?" She broke the eggs into the skillet and returned
it to the stove. She reached down two cups and plates
and brought out silverware from the table drawer. She
dished up while Thomas wiped his face, emptied the
washbasin, then slipped into his suit coat. He pulled out
a chair for her, then seated himself.

"You don't have to," she said.

"Have to what?"

"Have to wear a coat at breakfast. It's silly."

"No, it's not. A gentleman in the presence of ladies
dresses like a gentleman." He expected her to light
with pleasure, and was surprised to see her face darken.
What ails her, he wondered.

I'm dressed for working, not for being a lady, she
thought. My father never wore a coat to the table. So
you're saying he was no gentleman? You got a lot to
say against the dead, considering they can't defend
themselves. Her teeth clamped down and tore a crusty
corner from the bread she held, and as its nutty goodness wet and spread in her mouth, her anger left her.

He certainly didn't expect her to be all dressed up on a Monday, that wasn't what he said. Just that he had queer ways.

Thomas, who had chatted throughout the meal, kissed her good-bye and reached for his missal as he passed the living room table. "Want to come along? You could be the last one to get your wash out today, and offer it for the poor missionaries in Africa."

"Show off!" she retorted and hurried to get her laundry out on the washline before anybody else in the neighborhood. She worked furiously, rubbing collars and soiled spots with soap jelly, bailing hot water into the gasoline driven Cataract Washer. She flew down the porch steps to the backyard pump, and back and forth. Thomas had said once, "Don't make so much work for yourself, Lizzie. Use the pump at the kitchen sink."

"Humph!" she replied, "I'm not afraid of work." But she was afraid of thinking. "It wears me out," and she wasn't alluding to laundry chores but to what went on in the nuptial bed. She determined never to let any bed dirt escape into other parts of her home. So she gathered up bed linens carefully, folding corners toward the center, careful not to let germs escape. She carried sheets away from her body, not letting them brush against anything in the kitchen, to their own special empty carton in the summer kitchen. After towels and dishrags were washed and wrung out, she brought out the sheets and dropped them into the hot cleansing suds. It made her feel good to see those filthy sheets writhe and bellow and finally drown as she poked them underwater with a sawed-off broomstick. Then she fastened down the washer lid, pulled the long black lever, and listened with satisfaction as the Cataract dashed the sheets back and forth, back and forth. Now it was time to rinse the towels and put them through the wringers which crushed anything that got in their way as they tried endlessly to circumvent each other. As soon as the last towel fell into the clothes basket, she rushed with it to the washlines. She'd done it again. Up and down the block, across the wooden fences, there wasn't another woman out hanging. Nobody could say Thomas Davis' wife was lazy.

Thomas, on the first washday, had suggested she wait until she had a full basket before walking out to the lines. "Do I tell you how to run the store?" she asked.

"Touché," he answered. It was a word she never heard until she married. She didn't know exactly what it meant, only that he wouldn't argue further. It was one of his strange city ways. When Lil said things to prick Ed, he almost always gave her tit for tat. Sometimes the smallest engagement grew into a good-sized fight. They always ended with Ed apologizing to his wife, which, Lizzie reflected, is the way it ought to be.

She withdrew the last clothespin from her mouth and fastened the last corner of towel to the line, then decided to wash the breakfast dishes before taking the bed linens out of the washer; give 'em time to get really clean.

Fifteen minutes later she began to wring the sheets through the rollers. Any caution she showed was for the wringer and the occasional spurt of hot water that sprang from the creased sheets. The sheets themselves

54

did not worry her; they were redeemed, clean again. As she hurried the basket once more to the lines, Lizzie thought a lot about those sheets. They would be so white, so smooth, so pure—and then they'd end up in the bed again. Ugh! How did other women feel about it, she wondered. Not that she'd ever find out; there's some things you just don't talk about.

"Hello there, Mrs. Davis." It was Mrs. Martin, bringing out her first load. "Beat us again."

"Well," Lizzie said, trying to appear modest, "it's easier for me. I don't have hardly any wash."

"You've got plenty for just two people. You must be very clean, I tell my mister."

"But I don't have all the aprons and school dresses and shirts you have to soak. This week I don't have the mess of white rags I was expecting, either, so I'll get done early."

"You don't?" Mrs. Martin stopped abruptly and let a shirt hang in a wet clump over her line. She came over to the fence and cupped her hands about her mouth so that her voice would carry to Mrs. Davis and no further. "Didn't you come 'round this month?"

"No, I didn't, not yet."

"Bet you won't. Let me be first to congratulate you," and she rested her elbows on the cross rails, ready to initiate Lizzie into the exalted state of motherhood.

"Huh?" said Lizzie, and continued to hang sheets.

Mrs. Martin took no offense but returned to her own washlines. Come to think of it, she was real secretive about her first pregnancy, too. She chuckled to herself. Let Lizzie announce it when she was good and ready.

For herself, Mrs. Martin would play it prudent—maybe Lizzie was only going to be late. But when she does get kids, I hope she gets over crowding the underwear on the line like that. It doesn't fool anybody, we all know it's underwear, and it has to be all ironed if you don't give it a chance to billow in the breeze. Ah well, she'll learn to cut corners.

Lizzie returned to the house and put away the breakfast dishes as soon as she transferred the last batch of wash into the carrying basket. No need to hurry now. Hers was first out again. She raised her voice in song, unaware of any deliberate selection:

> "When morning gilds the skies,
>   My heart awakening cries,
>   May Jesus Christ be ever praised,
>   May Jesus Christ be ever praised."

The fire in the laundry stove was dead, the soap water had been carried out under the lilacs, and the Cataract shone like a huge copper jewel when Thomas returned for noon lunch. "Only pork and gravy on bread, yesterday's," she apologized.

"What do you mean, only?" He smiled at her and stroked the frown that was gathering above her brows. "Make it easy for yourself on washday."

Her face cleared. Thomas was really nice and appreciative. If only he didn't want . . . She cut the thought off. Time enough to think about that after supper. They said the Angelus together, then began their meal.

"Mighty good gravy, Lizzie. Fellow was in today,

from Milwaukee. City's really growing, he says. Got themselves cooler summers, wind's off the lake." Excitement crept into his voice and he played with a tough bit of fiber that he tore from the celery stick in his hand.

"Then winter's colder too, I bet. I heard about how windy it's in Chicago. Milwaukee's even north-er, ain't it?"

"A bit, but it wasn't the weather that I was going to talk about. The point is, immigrants are pouring off the boats at Ellis Island and . . ."

"Where?"

"In New York, where everybody lands that comes from Europe."

"Oh, them!"

Sometimes Thomas wished that his wife had more than a fourth grade education. He wrapped the celery string around his little finger and watched congestion set in. "Listen, Lizzie, these immigrants are not staying in New York and New Jersey like they used to. They're coming by the dozens to Milwaukee. There's jobs waiting for them in the industries. And you know what that means."

"What?"

"Why, what does anybody do when he goes for a job? These men fresh off the boats, they need decent clothes. You have to dress like an American to get a decent show when you apply for a job. You see what that means?"

"No, what?"

"It means a tailor or a haberdasher is the first place the immigrant is going to spend his money."

"What money? I thought you said he was looking for a job."

Thomas nibbled the edge of his moustache while he searched Lizzie's eyes, hoping to see a twinkle there. But no, she wasn't kidding. She had just dealt the death blow to the fortune he could make in Milwaukee. Well, he told himself, maybe not a fatal blow, just a setback. After all, he couldn't expect a bride of three months to relish too many changes at once. Women never did. He wondered if the best donkeys in the treadmill weren't always females.

"Well, anyhow, Milwaukee is quite the city. Water is piped in every home. Just turn on the faucet. No carrying, it just gushes out."

"Say now, is that true?" She leaned forward, really interested. "But what if they don't have enough rain for all those people?" She remembered how she and Lil had once carried water when the rain cistern went dry.

"They've got the whole of Lake Michigan, they should worry. There's always water if they turn on the faucet." He unwound the celery tourniquet and smiled as circulation resumed in his fingertip. He dropped the discussion. Give her time, she might come around to thinking the move to Milwaukee was her own idea *when*, not *if*, they moved.

Lil would have liked to keep a closer eye on her kid sister's marriage. "Thomas makes me edgy," she told Marie and sent her into town. "I'm too big now. You go."

So it happened that Marie was dropped off by Ed in

front of Lizzie's one late October day. As she walked up to the porch the stillness alarmed her. The front door was closed, the shades down. In the flower box, old blossoms hung dead on their stalks. Lizzie was always particular not to let the flowers go to seed so that they would keep blooming. The creeping jenny was rampant over the edges of the walk. Lizzie was always pulling it out—"It's not neat," she complained—but now it looked like it hadn't been pulled in weeks. Marie walked around to the rear. Maybe Lizzie was out back getting vegetables ready for supper. But Lizzie was not in sight. Walking through the summer kitchen, Marie called, "Hello, anybody home?"

There was a long silence, then from the bedroom came a quiet, "I'll be right out, Marie." The voice sounded flat. She came through the door and Marie saw how puffy her eyes looked and how her mouth sagged in discouragement. She must have been lying down, for wisps of black hair hung wantonly away from her hairline, and the thick pancake of hair atop her head was askew.

"The heat got you?" Marie asked and drew Lizzie's hand into hers. "No fever, your hand's all sweaty."

"I dunno what ails me. Maybe if I could ever get done I'd feel better." She tucked the stray locks upward and rearranged the hairpins somewhat while Marie looked on in a half-worried, half-amused way.

"You can't get done? Oh Lizzie, don't make me laugh. What can't you finish in this little house, just the two of you?"

"Yesterday I wanted to get the drapes out on the

line, it was so breezy. Air 'em and get a head start on my fall cleaning."

"Fall cleaning! Lizzie, you just moved in here four months ago. You don't have to do any heavy cleaning 'til spring."

"The yard looks messy, too. Thomas mows the lawn, but you know men. He doesn't trim around the shrubs. The creeping jenny is taking over my front walk."

To cheer her up, Marie asked, "Who's winning Monday mornings? You aren't letting Mrs. Martin beat you getting the wash out?"

When Lizzie answered dully, "She and just about everybody beats me now," Marie was really concerned.

"Come on now. You and me are going to sit down on the front porch and just talk. Tell me all about it."

"Can't. Nothing to tell. 'N I got to get started towards supper, no dessert fixed or nothin' and Thomas wants his big meal at night, you know."

"How is he?"

"He's OK. *He* never gets sick." She pulled a hankie from her pocket and scrubbed the end of her nose as if she were angry with it. Marie noted that the black eyes that could look shiny as hard coal were brimming with tears.

She said, "It's too hot to bake. We'll visit in the kitchen and I'll make a nice boiled pudding while we talk." She looked into the pantry. "You've got these nice cold potatoes, Lizzie. You peel and slice them. Dice up a bit of bacon first. I'll fry it out while I'm at the stove with the pudding. Wait a minute 'til I get the sugar and cornstarch and milk, then you sit right there and I'll stand right here. Supper'll get itself while we talk."

What'll I tell Lil? Marie asked herself. *What ails her?* She decided to listen very carefully and call in a doctor if necessary. Lil would have fits if Lizzie came down with something and her stuck out there on the farm.

"Now you say you can't get done, Lizzie. Why not?"

"Can't get started."

"You mean you're sick and tired already of keeping house? I know it's always the same old Monday wash, Tuesday iron, Wednesday . . ."

"I don't mean that. In the *morning*, I can't get started. I get up and everything's horrid. I almost die when the coffee begins to boil, the smell . . ."

A pleased smile came over Marie's face. It was lost on Lizzie, whose eyes were downcast as she peeled potatoes.

"But you do feel better by noon, don't you, Lizzie?"

"Sure, and I eat good. But Marie, I'm so tired again afterwards. I just about die, I'm so sleepy after lunch."

"Well, ever think about taking a nap?"

"In the daytime? When I'm not sick? I'd be ashamed." Lizzie looked her severest toward Marie, whose back was turned to the stove.

"Say, do you need any more rags than you've got, huh?" Marie seemed to be changing the subject.

"I don't think so. I got three or four old union suits—they make the best scrub rags. And I like old newspapers better than rags for polishing windows."

"I mean nice white rags. Should I tear up an old sheet for you?"

"Don't bother. I got four piles in my dresser drawer. Know something, Marie? I ain't used 'em since August."

A bit of bacon fat spit and jumped against Marie's hand. She adjusted the fire below the frying pan, gave the pudding another stir, and turned to Lizzie. She expected to see the smug look that women always assume when they drop a bombshell of gossip. Instead, she saw the bent head, the square, capable hands holding a potato, the knife methodically making slices. Well, she thought, well . . . she's all grown up now. I remember how she used to come running up from the barn or orchard and she'd be telling things before you could make out what she was saying, the funny kid. So now she's a lady and she springs her news on me like this! Two can play *this* game. So she said in her most casual tone, "What you gonna name him, Lizzie?"

"Huh?"

"You heard me. Or is it gonna be a girl?"

"Talk sense, Marie; is who gonna be a girl?" Lizzie reached for another potato and began to tear away the peel. Marie continued to watch her closely. Silence. Quite suddenly, just as she finished the potato, Lizzie figured out what Marie had just said. Her hands trembled, she dropped the potato and it rolled away from her. She did not stoop to retrieve it. She shoved her chair away from the table and came quickly over to the stove. Quite unaccountably, now that she was there, she felt shy. She turned back to the table, fussing at the paring knife, wiping gummy bits of cooked potato against the bowl's edge. Finally she spoke. "You mean, I'm *that* way?"

"Just as sure as God made green apples."

Lizzie sat down hard. "How can you be sure?"

"Look, when you feel like you do, that's morning sickness. When you want to rest, that nature's way to store up your energy—there's two lives in you. And when you don't come 'round, that cinches it."

Lizzie's face went white. She clasped her hands together on the table and laid her face in the V of her forearms. Her breath came in shallow jerks.

Marie patted her back. "You're not crying, say!"

Lizzie made no response, but sat there, a small defenseless body facing up to the inescapable. Her sister continued patting her, trying to comfort her with words. She pointed out that sooner or later, practically every married woman has children; that's to be expected. "It's a fair arrangement, Lizzie. Nothing's for nothing. That's how a woman pays for a home of her own and being her own boss." Lizzie's breathing smoothed out and Marie brought out her most appealing argument: "Wouldn't you just love a cute little boy of your own, somebody as funny and as smart as Mark?"

Lizzie brought up her head and slowly shook it. "No."

"Lizzie, what's the matter with you? You love Mark and I've seen you romping with him like you was kids together. Sure you want one of your own."

But the black head continued to shake denial, and with careful deliberation she answered, "I'm not ready to have children of my own."

"Sure you are; you're *having* one."

"I mean, *I'm* not ready, even if I am that way. It's a terrible thing, the responsibility. I don't want it."

"Oh, it can't be as bad as that. Thomas will see that nobody starves."

"Who's talking about starving? About bodies? Think I'm worried about not having enough to eat?"

"Well, what are we talking about?" Marie was losing patience and would have become quite angry except that Lizzie looked so much like a sad-faced beagle of Leo's, lovable but . . .

Lizzie explained. "I can play with Mark and have a good time with him. I ain't responsible for bringing him up, Ed and Lil are. They are the ones that answer to Almighty God if his soul is lost, not me. That's why I can enjoy him."

"Oh, Lizzie, how can you even think of that sweet little kid losing his soul? What sin could he commit?"

"All right, but he's gonna grow into a man, ain't he?"

Marie laughed, although Lizzie couldn't imagine why. "It's no sin to grow into a man."

"Fallen man," Lizzie corrected her.

"But the Bible says the heavenly Father cares for all, that no sparrow falls without his knowledge."

Lizzie had visions of a dead sparrow, all dust and loosening feathers, tiny lice stirring them, a maggot crawling from under one wing. She did not feel comforted. She changed the subject somewhat. "What about me? I have to fight with myself to get started every morning."

"That's just morning sickness. If you're almost two

months along, it's going to stop any day now. I promise you. Just put a cracker or two by your bed. Don't get up on an empty stomach, that's all."

"I feel tender here." Lizzie spread her hands across her breast.

"Just proves it. You're going to be a mother. You'll make a good one. Remember now, eat plenty. You're eating for two. You want milk for the baby, so eat good."

"Should I see Doc Schwemmer?"

"What for? You don't even show. If Thomas gets sick and sees him, you could go along. Or if you get sick, then be sure to tell Doc that you're expecting."

"Why did I have to get that way right now? Oh, I wish it would have waited 'til Lil was through with hers."

"Lil's OK. She'll be back in shape long before you'll need her."

"When am I due, Marie?"

Marie made a few rapid calculations, counted off nine fingers and announced, "May."

"When in May?"

"You have to count nine months forward and one week backward from the time you didn't come around."

Outside, a horse stopped his clip-clop in front of the house. The two women inside immediately stopped talking; they wouldn't want anybody hearing them in such a personal discussion. Footsteps on the front steps and Ed's cheery voice calling out, "You two talked out? I'm ready to get on home now."

"Come on in, Ed. First you're gonna have a cold lemonade with us."

He came into the kitchen, set aside his old straw hat, and made himself comfortable, tilting back the wooden chair. "How've you been, Lizzie?"

"Fine," she answered. "What's Mark been into lately?" Kids was the only subject she could think of at the moment. We'll talk about his. Lil can tell him about mine, but not 'til I show. She felt sudden kinship with Lil. We're both in this, "with child," as Thomas and the Bible liked to put it. She never heard a word of the tale Ed was telling her about Mark. She was thinking instead of the Virgin Mary and how once she was "with child." She sighed. Mary was lucky. She knew from the start that *her* Baby would turn out all right.

6. Thomas, usually so voluble, stood quiet in the darkened bedroom. In his two hands he held a bundle so small it scarcely covered them. Even though shades were drawn down to the edges of the partly opened windows, he could see the bit of brown fuzz on the tiny head, the milky pansy-blue eyes of his firstborn son. He lifted the bundle higher on his chest, careful not to drop it. He touched his lips to the fuzzy head and felt the reverence that came when he parted his lips for Communion. It was as still as a church in the bedroom, only the sound of Lizzie's breathing, deep and tired and somehow contented.

He moved to the bed and placed the infant in her bent arm, then he knelt close to her face. With his fingertips he placed a kiss on her forehead. He was afraid to touch her. A warm, sticky smell clung about the bedside mingling with the odor of darkening red roses on the bureau nearby. He wasn't sure how much she hurt and he wouldn't have jogged her for anything.

"Ah Lizzie, I love you! That is the most beautiful baby in the world and you did it. I knew you could. I knew you'd make a wonderful mother when I picked you."

Lizzie's eyes were soft as black velvet and she smiled happily. She made no reply, but patted the back of his well-groomed hand. It was a gesture of forgiveness: he hadn't asked to be a male, and after all, it *had* brought them this wonderful adorable baby.

The baby lay with eyes shut, and a smile flitted across his face. "The angels are kissing him," said Thomas.

"Maybe his very own guardian angel," Lizzie said. And she began a secret prayer to this particular angel. "He's a very special baby and our very first. Don't let harm come to him. Oh, I don't mean he mayn't get scratched and bumped. All boys do. I mean, don't let anything happen to his immortal soul."

The little bundle with the immortal soul screwed up his face then. A high-pitched, rubbery cry came from him. Thomas' face lighted with delight—his son's voice. Lizzie cradled the baby closer to her and looked with concern into the moist, red mouth.

Lil came briskly into the bedroom. "All right now, Thomas, you've seen enough. Lizzie's got to rest now. And that little man wants his dinner." She put a hand in Thomas' armpit and raised him quickly off his knees. He wanted to coax Lizzie to let him stay, to watch his son nuzzle, the lucky beggar. What a pair! No church Madonna with her pale skin and silken robes could match his Lizzie with his son. He looked down tenderly on the blackbird-wing brows, so serene now, the pink blush on her rounded cheeks, her square hands enfolding new life.

"She'll keep," said Lil. "That is, if you don't wear her out visiting now. Let her sleep." Thomas found himself outside the closed bedroom door. A rich tobacco odor floated through the screen door. He went onto the porch and found Doc Schwemmer there.

"Well, what do you think of him?"

"He's beautiful! He's wonderful! So's Lizzie," Thomas replied.

Doc laughed, then after a decent interval brought the subject around to professional services. "I was glad to deliver her. Lizzie was scared, but she's a real trooper. No bellyaching out of her. What she has to do, she does."

"Doc, I thought I'd have your fee saved up before the baby got here. But last week I ordered a shipment of shirts and it was C.O.D. I'm afraid I used your money."

"That's OK, Thomas. You pay me when you sell the shirts. Well, I better get a move on." He knocked the ashes from his pipe and turned to find Lil. "Any questions? he asked her. "You know how to manage?"

Lil bowed her blonde pompadour in a confident *yes* and extended her hand. "Thanks again, Doctor. Pierot girls wouldn't know what to do without you."

"Oh, I'd undoubtedly starve without the Pierots, the whole sickly lot of 'em." He laughed at his own joke and went out to his waiting horse.

Thomas turned to Marie, dragging a washtub toward the back door. "Here, let me do that."

"You get back to work. This is woman's." Thomas looked down at the pinkish water in the tub, the linens

69

soaking there. "That's heavy stuff. Let me drain the water off. Going to wash? I'll fill the boiler." Marie felt embarrassed. She didn't need a man around just now. Lil came from the kitchen.

"Listen, are you going to let Doc Schwemmer and the neighborhood ladies tell the news? Or are you going to get downtown and tell the fellows yourself?" She used the same blustering yet amused tone that worked so well with Mark. It worked with Thomas, too, who suddenly wanted to get back to the store. He went over to the sink, pumped a handful of water and slapped it over his face, drying his hands on his hair. Then he scritched-scratched a brush through his cement-colored hair and left for the world of commerce.

"Don't bother dinner. I'll get myself something," he told his sisters-in-law. "Just take good care of Lizzie." He left.

Marie laughed. "He's walking on air, he doesn't need food. But we do. What's it gonna be?" Lil was looking over the two rows of jars in Lizzie's pantry.

"Not too much here." She was used to seeing hundreds of jars in her cellar at home. Peaches, pears, applesauce. Chutneys, catsup, India relish. Tomatoes in chunks, tomato juice. Squat jelly jars, crowned with paraffin and covered with brown paper. Below the shelves, a pail of pears mellowing so they'd peel just right, a crock of dills with salty scum oozing beneath their wooden cover. And hanging from the ceiling, ready to smack a tall person, an oblong dark and leathery, hiding pink streaks and white fat bacon. "Let's leave the little bit she's got put away for themselves; I'll get the

Martin girl next door to get meat from the store." She scooped a dish of sulphured apple slices from a crock. "Apple pie?"

"Let's not roll pie crust. Make brown Betty. Leo's coming tomorrow for me and I want to get the washing done if we can."

"I'll see if Lizzie needs anything, then be right with you," Lil said. In a few moments she returned. "Honest, Marie, it makes me feel like a grandma almost. There's Lizzie sleeping like a pink doll and that wee mite cuddled at her side, his little fists all clenched up against his face."

"Maybe he's gonna be a fighter like his Grandpa Pierot." Marie chuckled. "Let's hope he doesn't take after his grandma—about worrying, I mean. His mother is getting to be a worrier, I'll tell you. You know, Lil, first thing when she found she was expecting, first thing, she was worrying about his immortal soul and he wasn't even born yet." She threw the lever on the Cataract and the ensuing noise made visiting impossible.

Thomas, on his way to the shop, reconsidered and came back. He passed his own house and went up the neighbors' steps. Mrs. Martin, lean, slightly soiled, but with a kind face, exclaimed, "Well Mr. Davis, what brings you here?" and to herself added, As if I didn't know, all except the sex. Lizzie's two sisters, Doc Schwemmer, Thomas Davis not at work, the terrible quiet in his house—Rose Martin had borne children too often not to know what was going on next door, but she was not going to spoil an important announcement.

"We have just had our firstborn, a son," said Thomas. "Mother and child are doing fine."

Mrs. Martin decided to overlook the *we*. For her money, it was the woman who had the baby, the man who did the preening. Still, poor things, you couldn't deny them their bragging a bit—they had so very little to do with birthing. "God bless you!" she said and meant it. "Is he a good size?"

Thomas held out two empty cupped hands. "Smaller than this, and the most precious thing in the world."

"Sure he is. Congratulations! You tell Lizzie I'll be over later with something for her."

"Thanks, but she's sleeping now. I'm on my way to work."

"Better not try any pressing today 'less you want to mend a scorch in some guy's trousers tomorrow," she teased.

"Well, I'll be getting on. I bear glad tidings of great news," he told her with a grin.

She stretched her mouth into what she hoped was a suitable smile. But that Thomas made her uncomfortable sometimes. Like now. Sort of quoting the Bible about himself—it was kind of indecent. Who'd he think he was, anyhow, a saint or something? Then she chided herself. He really was nice, not too different from any other guy, except he was cultured maybe.

With great strides, Thomas rushed down the street. He didn't feel like any other guy; he felt like a co-creator with Almighty God. He felt like St. George, ready to slay dragons for his short, plump Lizzie. He felt like a man of affairs: his own business establishment, his own wife, and now his own son. A corporation, an unbeatable combination!

He entered the store, not at all remarking the fact that the door was open and the shop unattended since he had left it hurriedly, early in the morning. He went behind a counter and brought out his ledger. Across the bottom four lines he wrote: "May 16, 1902. Born at 1 p.m. John X. Davis." The X did not stand for Xavier. It stood for Lizzie's choice of second names. He had, without arguing the matter, rejected her choice of first names. "Fredric" was all right for a Frenchman or anybody that wanted it, but it wasn't what he had planned for his sons. They were going to be Matthew, Mark, Luke, and John. He'd start with John, probably the one Lizzie would show least resistance to. No sense worrying ahead of time would she accept Mark and Luke. Matt, he knew, wouldn't give him any trouble, plenty of Matts in the German community around them. And maybe God would send all girls after awhile and Lizzie could name them all. But the boys were going to be named after the four evangelists. He'd get Father Schwartz to back him up if she bucked too much. That baby was too wonderful to name after her father. He closed the ledger suddenly. Shucks, practically nobody knew about his wonderful good fortune yet. He shoved the ledger into its drawer and headed toward the barber shop and people.

"You're looking at a brand-new father," he told the barber and the face steaming under hot towels.

"It's Davis," the barber told his customer. "Least it

looks like him, 'cept I never saw such a grin on any human. Boy or girl?"

"The world's most beautiful boy and his name is John. Mother and baby doing well. I'll get along now, just thought I'd tell you," but he made no move to go.

"Beautiful? Looks like the missus? He'd hate to look like his father," the barber joshed and Thomas retreated.

His next stop was the *Weekly Star* and straight to the cluttered desk of Mr. Brogan, editor-compositor-owner. A black-visor cap and steel-rimmed glasses hid his levity as he announced, "Sure, just in time for this week's headline. Three inches high and thick black."

"You do, and I'll buy two copies this week," Thomas cracked right back. He headed for his shop.

He picked up a fly swatter and had every intention of getting to work in a minute, when it occurred to him that the bank would be closing and he hadn't told Mr. Hellerman the good news. He had been avoiding him for two days, since according to his ledger his account was overdrawn a dollar or two. But shucks, no banker is going to bring up such a small matter when you are bringing in such momentous news. So he laid down the swatter and crossed the street to visit. The banker had just closed his window but seemed cordial enough. "Well, Thomas," he said when he heard the news, "I must congratulate you. And I'm going to open an account in your son's name. Drop in tomorrow for his savings deposit book. There'll be $1.00 on deposit for him." Mr. Hellerman cleared his throat as if to make ready for further announcement, then changed his mind. Nuts!

he told himself. Thomas is honest as the day is long and he'll catch on with more experience. Anyhow, this is the first time he's overdrawn.

Thomas returned to his shop feeling like a millionaire. Three bank accounts in one family—his checking account (he'd get it balanced tomorrow), his savings account, and now his son's account. Never mind that his savings account was almost as small as his son's. A fellow has to start somewhere. He promised to work diligently, to make a success of himself; not to pig, of course—a fellow needed only so much. But he'd make more than a bare minimum. They'd live decently, and when the time came, his son would be educated. He'd receive a sheepskin, wear a cap and gown. He laughed at the picture: the fuzzy head, a four-pointed cap skidding around on it, a sheepskin diploma all but burying little John. "The little lamb." He breathed it almost aloud. Then he laughed with deep contentment and did say aloud, "The Lord is my shepherd, I shall not want."

He went to the front door and looked up and down the street. Except for Mitzi, the barber's cat, and one young boy carefully plunking his bare feet down on every third board on the sidewalk, the street was deserted. There was no one to hear his good news. He went back into the shop and looked in the till. It was empty, except for the dollar he kept for change. He brought out his ledger, entered today's date. Under debts he entered "00.00." Under credits he made the same entry. As he put away the ledger, he smiled. "Who says figures don't lie? Today I am a millionaire." He locked up shop early. A man doesn't have a son every day.

Perhaps, had he been gifted with foresight, he might have kept the shop open for another two hours, hoping for at least one profitable transaction. Had he been superstitious, he might have objected to the juxtaposition of natural fertility and financial barrenness in the ledger of May 16, 1902. But Thomas, neither clairvoyant nor superstitious, went home early and happy.

He thought his sister-in-law a little cool in her greeting. "Early, aren't you?" Lil said. "Who's watching shop?" But he did not explain. There were the Marys and Marthas in every man's life. Lil was a Martha. He hoped to rescue Lizzie before her big sister's constant busyness would become Lizzie's way of life too.

7. Thomas struggled with himself for over nine years, then finally admitted that his wife was hopelessly, incurably a Martha too. Busy about many things. Certainly there were many things to keep her busy, but why did she insist upon being the eye of every household hurricane? Couldn't kids be left to work out anything for themselves? And help some? John (his middle name was Fredric) was going into fourth grade now. Why couldn't he register Matt for second grade and order Mary's speller and reader for first grade? But no! Lizzie made a great to-do having to get cleaned up on a weekday and get the kids readied for the fall term. Why couldn't she let some things go?

Which things? Well, some things. No, not Mary's hair. Every morning Lizzie dampened the hair brush and wound Mary's sausage curls over her finger, one by one. He wouldn't want her to stop doing that. Even Van Camp's daughter didn't have such a head of hair. But surely after Lizzie got the three off to school, then she could take it easy.

Not Lizzie. Three left at home, all babies practically.

Grace, going on four, needed constant watching. She liked to trail after the others and play on the school grounds. Once she filed into church when the bell rang. An indignant John returned her to Lizzie. "Mother, you've got to watch her better." Lizzie promised humbly enough that she would, but secretly she was glad of John's discomfiture. If little girls could annoy little boys, more power to them. The boys would tip the balance when they became men, and soon enough girls grew into defeated women. Look at me, if you don't believe it, she argued with herself: thirty-one years old and married ten years, torn away from my relatives, stuck with six children. Six. With Mary started to school this fall, by rights only Grace should be home with me. Home in Iowa, not here. She wrung out the dishrag and slammed it on the drainboard. Thomas was hard on her, much too hard. Smart enough to go to college, he was, but not bright enough to figure that too much was too much—yes, even when it's love you're talking about. And moving from Iowa had been the last straw. Terribly hot July when they'd moved. He was quick to point out how much cooler the nights were in Allistown when a breeze came off Lake Michigan. He was sleeping much better, he said, and it made her furious. Sleeping was the thing he did best after you-know-what; she hardly slept at all. Part of her insomnia was resentment that he slept, some of it was homesickness, and lots was on account of children. But maybe the most of her sleeplessness was on account of Thomas. He took what he wanted.

He had insisted on naming every one of the children.

He didn't fool her any when he had asked what she wanted to name the brunette baby girl born in September of 1906. He agreed when she said Mary. It was only after the baptism that she recalled that he had an Aunt Mary and probably meant to use that name all along. "Your choice," he said two years later. Some choice! He wanted Faith, Hope, or Charity, or Grace. Lizzie had never heard of such show-off names as the first three, so she settled for Grace. It troubled her a bit at first: she'd never heard of a St. Grace. But it was Father Brumbach's housekeeper's name, so it must be all right. The more she thought, the less she slept, no matter how hard she'd worked all day. Between her thinking and his snoring, it's a wonder she didn't die of exhaustion. She would poke him harder than necessary. "Quit snoring; I can't sleep." He would briefly waken, but soon the sounds intruded again, shallow at first, but gathering snorts and volume until it was as irritating as ever. "He doesn't know what he's doing to me," she said, and sometimes she wept; for my kids, she thought, having such a high-handed father.

He didn't keep his word and he got his way about naming the next baby, too. And the more she thought about it, the more vexed she became. She didn't mind having an *Irene*. A good saint's name. And Margaret made a good middle name. But Agnes! Why'd he have to tack on a third name? And why Agnes? Irene Margaret Agnes; initials: I.M.A. Lizzie, nursing the skinny, clay-colored little Irene, had looked down on the wizened face and asked softly, "I.M.A. Davis, is it something to be proud of?"

Little Irene Margaret Agnes let her mother down early in life. Lizzie had always known—maybe Lil had told her—that as long as a baby nursed vigorously, a mother wouldn't get pregnant again. But Irene didn't nurse vigorously and she cried so much that Lizzie consulted her doctor, who put Irene on a bottle. Busy as she was, Lizzie had to stop and make formula. She could have forgiven Irene that, if only she hadn't become pregnant again.

The day after Irene's first birthday, Ann was born. When Lizzie looked down at the tiny squared hands, the black-winged brows, the skin like a rose petal, she loved the new baby immediately. All her resentments turned toward the one-year-old. After all, it was Irene that caused the crowding, nobody else. If she would have nursed like all the rest of them . . . But no, Irene had to be different. With her clay-colored hair and her blue eyes, she even looked like her father.

Thomas' joy in his children was tempered with guilt that Lizzie was kept so busy. Several times he asked if he couldn't be more help. He was always repulsed. "This is woman's work," she would say. "You stick to yours." Or, "The biggest help you can be is to get some decent customers." He was stung. His customers were all decent; was it their fault they could not pay until they got jobs, or paid up the grocer first?

Thomas left the house early each morning and attended Mass before opening the shop. Lizzie liked the arrangement well enough. Get him out, he only liked to boss; she was the drone. She bore the kids; he named 'em. She did all the housework; he chose the location, moving from Iowa in 1908, forward to opportunities unlimited. Huh! Running away from debts, more likely. She'd said she wouldn't move, try and make me, and he said, "Call that doing God's will? Bible says, 'They shall leave father and mother and the two shall be one flesh.'" And he was shouting because he knew he was wrong. Still, the Bible did say . . . Anyhow, here she was. Wonder how he ever scraped the money together to move.

Refused by all his married friends, Thomas had gone to the one steady, hard-working bachelor he knew. Maybe Cletus could help. "I'm not located right. This is farming community. Up in Allistown, they've bought up two hundred acres of farmland and they're building a huge factory. The place is going to be one beehive soon. They're going to want clothes and more clothes. People coming in, they're putting up new schools. It'll be a wonderful place to raise children."

Cletus said very little, but lent Thomas enough to buy fares for Lizzie's family and ship her household goods to Allistown. Thomas thought Cletus did it for the 5 percent interest he offered. Cletus was sure he would never see his money again. He doubted Allistown was the promised land, but hoped he was wrong. He wanted Lizzie located in the land of milk and honey. Thomas had never explained to Lizzie where the money had come from and she stopped asking when he got sharp with her. But she wasn't taking back what she said. He did run away from debts and their relatives—

"And my relatives are the only true friends we have."

With this Thomas did not agree. Friends were everywhere, just for the making. He went about seeking new cronies, joyous as a pup snuffing tree trunks. Nor did he let business interfere with friendship. When the banker refused him a loan, Thomas thought it reasonable and continued to enjoy the banker's companionship. When the landlord pressed him, Thomas went to the homes of two or three immigrants who might be able to pay something on their accounts. He never thought ill of the landlord for needing his rent, nor did he resent any who promised in broken English that "Next veek, I haf for you, maybe."

Thomas could not understand why Lizzie should feel so cut off from society. True, she couldn't visit Lil and Marie and all the other relatives. Iowa was too far away and trainfares too expensive. But the women did write back and forth and eventually settled into a round robin: Marie wrote to Lizzie, who answered, sending along Marie's letter, mailing both to Lil. Lil's letter, always the longest, was written below Lizzie's, then forwarded to Marie, who discarded her first missive and eventually wrote another addressed to Lizzie.

"You probably know more about each other this way than if you visited personally," Thomas once said.

"It ain't the same and you ain't going to make me like living away from my people, so you just be quiet," said Lizzie. That was the day Mary and Grace were soaking in the bathtub in a baking soda solution. Thomas had heated the water and carried it to the tub before he left for seven o'clock Mass. "It'll keep them from scratching. You don't want chicken-pox scars on the girls," he told her, "and all you have to do is pull the cork when they want to come out."

Lizzie would have been happy to pump the water and heat it on the kerosene stove and empty a galvanized tub later, if only the pump and stove and tub were in Iowa. She missed her sisters. And how nice if she could joke with Ed and visit with Leo. Sometimes in spite of herself, she thought of Cletus. When she did, she asked forgiveness, for *what* she wasn't sure. Either impure thoughts or coveting thy neighbor's goods—she sure wished to God that it was Cletus supporting her and the kids.

Thomas was amazed that anyone could miss Iowa that much. He urged her to join the Home & School Society. "It'll be good to meet other people."

"Alone?"

"Well, I get to see people all day. Want me to ask Mrs. Van Camp to stop by for you?"

"I'll go alone," Lizzie decided quickly. Mrs. Van Camp wore stylish hats and kid gloves and scared Lizzie to death. Not that she envied her. The Bible says it's easier for a camel to go through a needle's eye than for a rich man to go to heaven. That probably went for women too, and Mrs. Van Camp was the banker's childless wife. Why should she enjoy eternal happiness; wasn't she getting her full share on earth?

When Lizzie entered the school, it was Mrs. Van Camp who sat behind the card table and took dues. Very cordially she invited Lizzie to find a seat and expressed hope that she would come regularly now.

"Depends," Lizzie said and went into the auditorium. She found plenty of vacant chairs and almost panicked at the necessity of choosing one. Down front, I'm so short? She shuddered at the idea of walking way down there. Stay in back? What if somebody taller . . . everybody's taller. She chose an aisle seat near the back.

The meeting began with a prayer, then Father Brumbach introduced the officers (they were all women) and hoped for good attendance this year. A lady with a toothy smile read the financial report. Lizzie forgot to listen; she was watching the cords in the lady's neck jiggle against the string of pearls there. The jiggling stopped, then the lady at her right read minutes of the previous meeting. Then some mumbo-jumbo about "accepting" and then Madam President asking, "Any old business?" All around, Lizzie saw women telling secrets in their neighbor's ear, the back of a hand channeling gossip away from the lady in the row ahead. Wish Lil was here, Lizzie sighed.

"Any new business?" The president knew they'd gossip all night if she let them. Everyone sat silent. To stir at a time like this was to be put on a committee. "Father Brumbach, may we hear from you?" Maybe you can get 'em to stick to business.

Father came right to the point. "Any suggestions to raise money? Come, we mustn't keep our program chairman waiting; our speaker's ready." Father looked around. "Well now, to get on, I'm asking Madam President to appoint a committee of three to work on fund raising." He sat down.

"Any volunteers? No? Then let's have nominations from the floor." Madam President's smile was too toothy to be genuine.

A tired, red-faced woman nominated Mrs. Van Camp for chairman. Lizzie in her innocence assumed that Mrs. Red-face was complimenting Mrs. Van Camp. Mrs. Van Camp knew better. Last year, she had nominated the red-faced lady (her name was Mrs. Murphy) to be in charge of solicitations. Reprisal. The undercurrents made Lizzie nervous and she mopped her palms with her handkerchief, then noticed two damp patches on the bosom of her navy blue voile. In a frenzy of embarrassment, she bolted from the auditorium and hurried home. "That poor baby Ann, she's probably starving," she scolded herself.

She found the baby propped on a sofa pillow, Thomas next to her with Emerson's *Essays* in one hand and in the other, a tit of bread, sugar, and milk wrapped in muslin secured with string. The bread nipple was flattened and quite dry, as if Ann had enjoyed it thoroughly.

"She cry long?"

Thomas' eyes danced. "Who's crying?"

"She cried, or why's she out on the davenport?"

"For company."

"No more for me. Tiring, no good for the milk."

"You always get overtired washdays. What say I stay home Mondays?"

"Absolutely not. I got my own ways." Killing germs took time and she wasn't going to be hurried. So Thomas went day after day to the shop where business was so light, trying not to think of how heavy Lizzie's workload was. Eventually he succeeded.

8. After her one social fling, Lizzie retreated to her home, her citadel, where she enjoyed doing battle against the world with its innovations and sinfulness. Insofar as she was able, she kept her children to herself; nobody was going to say she didn't know what her kids were up to. She taught John and Matt to make rubbings of the dining chair backs and of pennies and nickels. She smoothed the butcher wrappings and drew whopping big horses, complete with green-ribboned braids. And cats. "Wish I was a cat," she remarked once.

"Why?" Irene asked. She was four and full of Whys.

"Wouldn't have to face the Last Judgment." I can't learn 'em much, but I can bring 'em up in the fear of the Lord. More than some of my neighbors are doing. At the start of summer she declared, "There's gonna be no bumming around. You can have friends but it's gonna be in your own yard and house." Later she complained to Mrs. Mantey "It ain't hard raising your own kids, it's the neighbors' wears me out."

Mrs. Mantey wasn't too sympathetic. "Then why do you do it, Lizzie?"

"So I know my kids' friends and what they're up to." Once the kids built a tent, two old blankets thrown over a washline. She made them take it down and move it. Relocated, it was open to her view. "I don't like boys and girls together unless I can see right through," she said but not to the children. She didn't believe in putting notions in their heads.

Rainy days could be more fun than sunny ones in the Davis household. Rain slowed down Lizzie's compulsion to clean and gave her time to play, although she called it by a different name, "Keeping 'em amused." They brought out old catalogs, and while the boys cut the windows and doors in a shoe box, eight-year-old Mary supervised the selection of curtains and furnishings for the new house. Other times they made cookies so overfloured and overhandled that they were tough as the mud pies made in sunny weather. If Thomas should come home early, Lizzie would quickly turn to some household task, scolding about the litter that lay about. It puzzled the kids, too young to notice that their parents seldom, if ever, played together. If asked about it, Lizzie would have explained the fable of the Ant and the Grasshopper. She was afraid that for Thomas to catch her at play would be a setback to any industrious resolutions he might have made. How could she continue to pray, "God give him some ambition and a decent-paying job," if meanwhile she played? Better she should set him a good example.

But Thomas never got the message, and when he

prayed it was not, "God make me an industrious father," but rather, "God make Lizzie a jollier woman." And he added, "Hurry and listen, God. I wouldn't want the kids to be neurotics. I pray especially for Irene. Amen."

Irene also called upon God. She needed forgiveness, for *what* she wasn't quite sure. Ages ago it happened and stopped so suddenly by her mother's appearance that she could only remember Mother's shocked voice saying over and over again, "You dirty thing, you dirty thing." And "God will punish you," although maybe that was said to the Henning boys. No, must've been her, 'cause He had. She was the only kid in the house that wet the bed and she was four. If only she could forget the dry hot do-nothing day when she was leaning against the washline post and Joe Henning next door was wetting the current bush that grew near their alley. He was almost hidden there, but she heard his brother Paul say, "I can shoot farther than that," and she walked toward the alley to see if he could. Paul had already unbuttoned his fly; now he paused to consult Joe, who was authoritative and six. "Should we let her try too?"

Joe answered promptly, "Naw, girls can't pee worth prunes."

The answer infuriated Irene, who up to this moment had never given the subject matter much thought. "I can go just as far as anybody," she said so loudly that it had to be true.

"Put up or shut up," Joe invited her.

Irene lined herself up beside Paul while she tucked her panties under one arm.

"Go!" said Joe, and Irene and Paul went.

"Jiminny!" Joe's exclamation was as awed as the "Aah, Gee!" that went up with the fireworks on the Fourth of July. "She wet the leaves, least the bottom ones."

Paul and Irene did not hear him. Mrs. Davis' voice filled the entire backyard at that instant. She was saying You Dirty Thing and God Will Punish You and all sorts of things, but she was yelling too loud and all at once. The boys ran down the alley and Irene ran into the house, her mother's voice like a lash cutting at her. She ran upstairs and hid.

When her father came home at noon, Irene heard her mother, all excitement, telling on her. She heard his calm, reassuring voice, although she didn't hear his words. Then her mother's voice again, upset and angry: "I didn't *think* you would. Men!" Then after a great deal of scolding, her mother's demand: "The least you can do is talk to the snot."

"Irene," he corrected her.

"I.M.A. Davis peeing around like a farm animal, and her father saying I make mountains out of molehills."

Thomas climbed the stairs and went in to the girls' bedroom. He walked over to the closet where Irene was hiding and spoke quietly. "Don't you want to come out? I want to say something. I don't bite."

Irene came from below the row of school dresses and Sunday coats. Here eyes were swollen with crying and her two small fists dug into them. Thomas sat on the edge of Mary's bed and drew her into his lap. "Irene, there's too much growing up to do when you're four. It's hard. Too much at once. So you make mistakes. You have to do some things before you find out they weren't such good ideas." He stroked her clay-colored hair. "Grown-ups don't show their private parts and they don't urinate in front of each other. At school, they have separate bathrooms marked Boys and Girls. Try to be a lady, but don't feel bad if you don't learn it all in one day."

He went downstairs and Irene heard her mother's voice. "Ain't you even going to lick her?"

His answer was too quiet for Irene to hear. "Wish you'd use your head instead of your tongue sometimes, Lizzie." He ate quickly; he ought to get back to the shop. Maybe Tony Czarnecki would come in with a payment on his new suit as he promised. At any rate, his presence at home seemed only to irritate Lizzie. Give her time and she'll see it was nothing but kids being kids. He left.

Lizzie watched his retreat. "Men!" Then she thought of the four-year-old with the blue eyes, pale hair, and latent amorality. "That one I'll have to watch; the poor kid takes after her father." As she moved to the bottom of the stairs, she breathed a short prayer to Jesus' mother to intercede for her. "Irene, come down," she yelled. "You can have the last piece of the apple pie." She added, "You're the skinniest," in case any explanation was needed.

9. Irene was now six and finding out that growing up was just as hard as her father had predicted. Her bed was lumpy, heavy with the odor of age and accidents. Her feet were ice and the ugly shadows on the walls were threatening. The ragman was coming after her again. "Make sense," she told herself. "That's only dirt and peeling paint." And the paint leered at her and said, "If I'm only paint, what are you so scared of?" She stared hard at the electric globe hanging out in the street, then shut her eyelids and poked a finger against each eyeball. Red squiggles, then yellow globs, floated milkily across the stage, brighter and brighter, breaking into a million squares against a black wooliness. Then fade, fade.

She opened her eyes. The ragman sniggered. Irene sighed, almost whispered. "If the gas light was on, see where you'd be, you. When we're sick, Mother lights the gas fixture and poof! to you. Keeps it on all night so she can wait on us if we're sick. Not so glary as the 'lectric. Wish it was on. Maybe if I prayed? Or if I got sick? She'd come up with the matches if she knew I was sick.

Gosh, I better go down and tell her. Sounds like she's in the kitchen. Bet that's Father she's hollering at. She's got a right to, she says. Nobody but a show-off calls their baby I.M.A. Davis and he's always got to be different. And he says his Lizzie's a good woman, utterly devoid of a sense of humor, whatever that means."

She left her bed, stepped the length of icy Congoleum hall runner, and came down the first three stairs. She paused on the landing, best spot in the house for listening, better even than the lower cupboard in the pantry. She could hear every bitter word:

"Not that it does any good, but I'm asking again. Just two steady dollars a day is all. Ask the neighbors. Do they keep their kids in clothes with a treadle machine? Who makes bread every day but me, with a store right on the corner? We'd starve if I didn't can. Start with rhubarb in the spring, stop when I'm ready to drop with the first snow, I'm so tired. Colander thin as a veil from all the bushels of apples I've strained through it. I cut rotten spots out of peaches and can 'em 'til it's a wonder I don't rot. I work hard to maintain this family and . . ."

Oh, that again! Irene knew it start, middle, and never a finish. Something about lilies of the field, too. "They aren't lilies, they're kids. And you better make up your mind to toil and spin, Thomas Davis." Nothing that Mother minded her hearing, so she came down into the kitchen where Mother was sitting heavily near the cellar door. Father was leaning against the drop-leaf table that so irritated Mother. It was higher than other people's, bought second-hand by Father from a dry-goods store that was putting in counters. "Anybody else, they go to a furniture store," Mother had fumed.

"Commercial, it'll last forever. Not flimsy," Father had replied and Mother said she could just kill him. She was saying it again.

Without missing a syllable, Mother shifted in her chair to let Irene get behind her where the hot air register cut into the wall. Father nodded to her, then returned his gaze to Mother. He didn't speak, but chewed the edges of his sandy moustache. Mother's voice rose louder and louder.

"When am I going to see more money around here?" She turned toward Irene just in time to clutch the little one's nightgown away from the wainscoting above the register. All winter, sap oozed from the wood paneling above the heat. Not enough to do something about it, just enough to drive a body crazy. "When will you get going? You *know* you don't make enough on your own. Why do you have to be your own boss?" She glared at him, not expecting an answer. That was his most aggravating trick. He never answered back anymore. Never.

Irene watched as he drew away from the table. There was no hurry or anger in his gait. He opened the door and descended into the cellar. Probably now he'll put on coal and we'll go to bed. Better tell her now about being sick; no matter how mad and tired she is, she's always sorry if you're sick. But before she could say it the right way, Father was tromping up the stairs and she could see the smooth oaken handle, the dull ax head, and the bright steel cutting edge on the heavy tool he brought with him. He advanced toward the chair where Mother was sitting. Irene pushed backward into the wall. A gummy spot glued her nightgown to her skinny buttock; a red-hot register handle stung the calf of her leg. She never thought to run. Father carried the ax in both hands. The sharp cruel edge that cut so deeply lay beyond his left hand. The curvy part of the wooden handle, smooth as a neck, was grasped in Father's right hand. It was worse than the pictures on the walls upstairs. Those giants weren't real and the ragman never caught the children. But this was Father. And Mother. And real.

Now he stood over Mother. She was silent at last. She made no move. To Irene, she seemed utterly fearless. Quickly, before Irene could cry out her scream, Father shifted position. He dropped upon both knees, stretched his neck forward, and placed the ax upon Mother's lap. "Lizzie, I'm no good and I'll never bring home a steady paycheck from a factory. As you say, I'm unbearable. If you're as smart as you say you are, Lizzie, you'll do away with me right now."

Irene never knew that old people could move so fast. Mother sprang from her chair, tumbled the penitent to the floor, and threw the ax down the cellar stairs. She was furious. But Father hadn't hurt her, had he? Then what was she so mad about?

Irene looked over to where Father still lay on the floor. His arms were crossed over his ribs, like he was hugging himself. His mouth was shaped in a big "Ho, ho!" but not a sound came out. Was there something to laugh about? She looked into his eyes, searching for answers. Father's left lid came down slowly over the eyeball. It was like a wink, but it couldn't have been. What ailed him? Maybe Mother could tell her. Dare she ask?

She looked over to Mother, backing away from the stairwell. White blotches gleamed over Mother's knuckles round the doorknob. Irene sucked in her breath and waited. Mother slammed the door hard, so hard that a powder of dust rose between door jamb and wall. Irene saw Father wince. Then he sucked the edge of his moustache.

Irene felt terribly confused. The coals in the furnace had been steadily sending up hot air and she hadn't moved from her spot in front of the register. Her legs began to itch with heat. Two spots behind her knees felt puffy and tender.

I can't stand it another minute. Run, run quick before she turns around, before he gets up off the floor.

She went quickly up the bare steps. She crossed the icy hall runner. Her feet didn't touch the bedroom floor more than once or twice. Then she was in bed with piping hot legs and buttocks thawing the bed-sheets. She was burning inside. Shame? Terror? The giant ragman brushed away a shadow on his face and leered. *I mustn't look! I mustn't think!* She pulled the old quilt over her face, squeezed her index fingers over her eyelids, hard, hard. The red squiggles formed, the yellow globs floated, shimmered, then sparkled and ran wet into the quilt. She had no idea she was crying; she was warm, wasn't she?

10. "It ain't fair. They ask for your opinions then mark you wrong if it ain't their opinions." They were gathered around the dinner table and Grace was speaking.

"You've got to think for yourself," Thomas said. "Pass the potatoes."

"Or you can quit being so different and think like other people once in awhile. Get the gravy going," Lizzie commanded. "By the time we were married ten years, I thought I was sick of ground beef. Now I wish it was more ground beef and not so much gravy."

"It hasn't been all gravy, twenty-three years," Thomas mused. "Certainly been productive, though."

"Married this long, what we got to show? Four girls still in school, a old house that you can't keep payments up on, a shop you still rent."

"You certainly haven't a business head . . ." Thomas began.

"So the pot's calling the kettle black."

". . . or you'd know paying interest on the mortgage is much cheaper than renting a house. Not that renting's a disgrace. Don't have to pay real estate taxes on the shop." He wiped his lips, drank his coffee, and reiterated, "You've got to think for yourself."

Irene hoped he was right, although she remembered a couple of times when thinking for herself had only brought embarrassment. Once when her family picnicked with all the Delaneys, and her mother and Mrs. Delaney hadn't paid any attention to three-year-old Tommy, they were so busy talking. Irene was nine at the time and felt very mature as she interrupted: "He's got to go. Want me to?" and she took him to the big washroom a hundred yards away. She headed toward the door marked Ladies, then it occurred to her that that was an unthinking thing to do: it was Tommy wanted to pee, not a lady. She very capably took his hand and led him into the end of the building marked Gentlemen. The patrons reacted like anything but gentlemen. "Ya dumb bunny, get out!" and "Can'tcha read, idiot!" and "Scram, stupid." They bellowed so loud that her folks and all the Delaneys were roused, and they all saw her and Tommy coming from the Gentlemen. Mother came scolding, but Father listened while she explained. He said she had acted quite sensibly. "At least, you thought first, a good habit. Disastrous sometimes, but still . . ." His eyes were smiley, but, "That one's gonna give me trouble," she remembered her mother telling Mrs. Delaney. "To much like her Pa."

"There's worse," Mrs. Delaney had replied. But Mrs. Delaney didn't know everything about Irene. Like the time she made Sister Dolorosa so mad. Sister had a sign thumbtacked over the blackboard: Keep Smiling.

So one day Irene decided that she would, although she was sure it was rotten advice. Classes began with morning prayers. She smiled. Catechism, and they talked about Moses and the plagues and while the angel killed off all the firstborn babies in the Egyptian households, she kept smiling. Next arithmetic; they passed up their homework and Irene smiled while Sister scolded the two boys who hadn't done theirs. At recess when she spilled some milk she kept smiling. During reading, Sister called on Pug Murphy who made a million mistakes and Irene kept smiling. And she kept smiling when the noon bell rang and the class began the Angelus. "The angel of the Lord declared unto . . ."

Sister swooped down from her desk, one hand reaching toward smiling Irene in a most business-like way. "You quit that insane grinning or I'll swat you," she said. Irene turned off her smile, all happy inside; she was right, it was a dopey sign. But at the end of the month, she had to explain her "C" in deportment to her furious mother. "I only kept smiling."

"Smart-aleck. Happy you made a dummy out of Sister?" But, "No harm done," her father had said. "An experiment." Did God allow experiments? She hoped so. On the wall behind Sister's desk had been a picture that made her eyes water and her soul cringe. A black triangle with a black circle inside it. "The Eye of God," Sister said. "Three sides, Father, Son, and Holy Ghost. Sees all." Irene was only able to live with it by convincing herself that He also understood all.

"Irene, quit piddling with your potatoes and gravy. Can't you pass things?" Irene set down her fork and handed the beans to Mary. "Pa, it doesn't always pay to think for yourself. The teachers don't like you, if . . .

"Who doesn't like you?"

"I only got 89 in English. Mrs. Wolf. And my home-room teacher says she's disappointed in me. 89's good. And when I gave my speech about college for women, some of the girls clapped but old Versage said it ought to have more facts."

"Mister Versage. Why stop at 89's? You're capable of Excellent." He smiled encouragement at his only blue-eyed daughter, the one with the finest brains in the lot. She didn't smile back. Instead she whined.

"Other people don't always have to do Excellent. Miss Whipple forgets to take roll and Mr. Delaney comes late to class. Old Foxy falls all over Violet when she gets 80. 'Tain't fair. Why do I have to be perfect?" Her eyes filled and her mouth trembled.

"The father with two sons. Did he rejoice in the satisfaction of the good son? Not like he whooped it up when the prodigal returned. Same with you. We're pleased even when we forget to say so."

Irene hiccupped and her tears of self-pity spilled over.

"Hey," Thomas said, "things can't be that bad. Coming down with something?" She was. The next day Irene was hot and feverish, and Lizzie, putting a hand against the red cheeks, ordered her back to bed and spent the day worrying.

"They make 'em take warm showers, then go into that cold swimming pool, then don't give 'em time to dry before they send 'em home." Lizzie was suspicious of all high school learning for women. She would have feared for her daughters' immortal souls had she known about Biology, where they learned about Reproduction —Chapter III. But what she didn't know didn't concern her. Swimming she did know about, and she hated it for women. It offended her modesty. Not the gray tank suits—they were so homely that they must be virtuous. But the Other Thing! Every swim period, the girls who had "come around" for that month stayed dressed and reported to the physical education teacher, who excused them from swimming, but kept them in the damp natatorium to observe. Not only did Lizzie object to "the sick girls in that damp"; she objected strongly to having freshmen innocents learning before their time about the "monthlies." Gym teachers had no finer feelings. Well, what else could you expect of a woman that went around in a bathing suit with a whistle around her neck? They weren't normal women, face it.

So now Irene was sick and if she got well, Lizzie would have to write an excuse. "Please excuse Irene's absence. She was ill and I kept her in bed." The fool physical education got 'em sick and the mothers had to apologize.

A lot education did for anybody anyhow! If Pa, now, hadn't gotten so smart he could work for the big factory and bring home a check like all the Stupids in the neighborhood. If Irene got worse, we'd call a doctor and see what's wrong, if—here she banged the iron frying pan into the dispan—if we weren't so darned educated and so darned poor. She sprinkled a smidgen of Kitchen Kleanser in the pan and bore down with her muscular right arm. Did swimming do anything for strength where a woman wanted it? I doubt it, she thought. Mary, Grace, Irene—they all used too much scouring powder and not enough elbow grease. Ann was the baby, you couldn't expect much. Teach 'em canning. That'd make sense and they'd develop muscle before they'd screwed on their thousandth mason jar lid. Swimming! Let's just hope she doesn't get pneumonia from this. She began to hum in a minor key one of her favorite hymns:

> "Oh come unto the olive grove;
> See Mary calls us to her side,
> 'Oh come and mourn with me awhile
> Jesus our Love is crucif . . .'"

Her voice, sweet and true and plaintive as the mourning dove's, broke suddenly, alert to a sound coming from the bedroom upstairs. Irene was retching. Lizzie grabbed the washbasin from its nail, tore down the hand towel, and rushed forward and up. "I'm coming!" She charged into the room just as a sour slimy mess burbled from Irene's mouth.

"Sorry, Ma." Irene's head hung over the bedside.

Lizzie cupped her hand against Irene's forehead. "It's OK. Lay your head in my hand. Let it come up. You'll feel better. What is it?" she asked, peering closely at the vomitus.

Irene didn't know if the question pertained to last night's dinner or to disease, nor had she any intention of answering. In a minute she lay back exhausted and Lizzie wiped her mouth and pushed back her bangs.

"Your eyes don't look right. What did you catch?"

"Just lemme sleep, Ma. I'm tired." Irene pulled up the sheet. Lizzie arranged the bedding and folded the towel over the top edge near Irene's head. From the bathroom she brought an old wooden stool and placed the washbasin on it. She sat down on the opposite bed to await Irene's recovery. From her apron pocket she drew out her rosary. Before she had fingered three beads, she dropped it back into her pocket. She had forgotten to spread some newspapers below the stool. She brought some and arranged them, then settled once more on the bed. She drew out her beads and was about to resume her prayers. But first, hadn't she better examine her patient? "Stick out your tongue," she ordered.

Irene stuck it out, but it offered no clues.

"Open your mouth wide. Pant like a dog." Lizzie had heard Doc Newton say that once. Irene opened her mouth. She panted. Lizzie peered in and dimly saw pink masses on each side of Irene's throat. "They supposed to be that color?" she asked nobody in particular.

"Ma, lemme sleep." Irene said it without rancor. It was touching, sort of, to see how Ma worried.

"If he knew how to support us, I'd get the doctor in a minute," Lizzie fretted.

Irene was touched at her mother's concern, but also grateful that they couldn't afford a doctor with his flat wooden sticks gagging her throat. It was sore enough from puking. She dozed off, thinking kindly of her improvident father.

She awoke when her mother's work-roughened hands

scratched against her chest. "I'm just unbuttoning
you."

"What for, Ma?"

"Gonna rub your chest."

"Oh Ma, no! Not with that stinking turpentine!"

"Ya wanna get well or don'tcha?" Even to Lizzie, it
sounded belligerent. She softened her voice. "Got to be
up and doing, if you're going to be in the Forensics
contest." She took a small jar of turpentine from a
saucepan of hot water and poured a bit onto her horny
hand. Then she spread it on Irene's chest and began to
rub it in.

"Not so hard, Ma."

"If I don't rub hard, you say I'm tickling."

"I'll lie quiet, honest I will. Just go softer."

"Your thoat OK?"

Irene lied. "Fine." Anything was better than having
to gargle with the evil-tasting purple-red stuff Ma be-
lieved in.

"Belly hurt?"

"My stomach's fine now," Irene said.

"We'll see. I'm watching. Call me when you go to
the bathroom."

Irene was outraged. Ma always minded everybody's
business; there were simply no limits when you were
sick. Lizzie continued her rhythmic scritch-scratch on
Irene's chest, reaching down on her sides over her
lower ribs.

"Not so hard, Ma. Why grease me? My chest is OK."

"You're hot, and you say your belly's OK. If your
throat doesn't hurt, what else is there? You're hotter

than a stove. Somewhere there's infection." She continued to rub until Irene's chest was rooster red. Then she covered the girl with old flannel rags, and buttoned up her night gown. Irene shut her eyes and soon heard her mother's careful footfall on the steps. She was taking her old turpentine and the saucepan downstairs. Presently she was back again.

"You've got to eat to keep up your strength. Here's hot cornmeal mush and some nice beef gravy. I'll put Mary's and Grace's pillows under you, then you can eat."

Irene allowed herself to be propped up, but when she began to eat, it all tasted like turpentine and she found she wasn't the least bit hungry. Lizzie watched her anxiously and even tried to steer a few spoonfuls into her mouth.

"Don't, Ma. It just doesn't taste good."

"It's prefectly good. We all ate it. Nobody else complained."

"I mean, I just ain't hungry. I don't want anything, Ma."

Just then Thomas stuck his head in the door. "How's the sleepyhead? Suppertime and you've been in bed all day. Loafing?" He gave Irene a wink. She saw it, but just didn't have the pep to joke with him. Her mother saw the wink too, and flashed an angry look toward him.

"There's nothing to get cute about. This girl's sick and I don't know what with. Her fever just shot up awful this morning. We'd have a doctor by now, if things were what they should be."

"If what things were . . . How should they be?" Thomas asked, his temper sharpening.

"You know what I mean perfectly well." Her dark eyes glared at him, then filled with tears. "I'm worried. She didn't cool off all day, just slept."

"She'll probably sleep it off; give her a good night's sleep."

"What if she gets worse? We ought to have Doctor see her now. I won't sleep a wink all night worrying."

"I'll use the cot downstairs so Mary and Grace can use our bed, then you can sleep here," Thomas suggested.

"They stay here. I ain't sleeping." She would have stood all night in a corner before she would allow her young daughters in a married couple's bed, vacated or no.

Thomas foresaw a night of bustling and worrying and, worst of all, nagging. He had come upstairs cheerfully enough to assure Irene that she would be "full of muckets and diddle-berries tomorrow"—their code for feeling wonderful. Now as he looked at her flushed face and the mulish, determined-to-worry look on Lizzie's, he gave in to his wife. "Well, get Doc Newton over here before it gets any later, then. We can't be up all night."

"Oh yes we can," Lizzie argued.

"I thought you wanted a doctor." Thomas was genuinely puzzled.

"I do, but not when we don't pay him. We still owe for Ann."

Thomas chewed the edge of his moustache. "Lizzie, you make up your mind once and for . . ." He got no further. Irene was retching again. Lizzie rolled her over to the edge of the bed, cradled her hot forehead, and placed the basin below her face. As she crouched tenderly over her daughter, Lizzie shot a look of scorn at her husband. "This kid needs a doctor."

"I doubt it, but since you're the nurse, you decide." Thomas was so angry it was making him dizzy. Here he'd put in a decent day's work, he'd come upstairs to see his sick daughter and commiserate with her, and Wham! he was right in the middle of one of Lizzie's tempests. Did she think he was some kind of monster that liked his kids to be sick? Or that everything that didn't go right was his fault? "You send Grace or Mary for the doctor," he stormed.

"I wouldn't have the nerve. Asking him, when he knows darn well he'll never see his money. Where's your pride?"

"Woman, where's your humility? You think a doctor would take it out on a child that the family owes him on account? Or you too stuck-up to take favors when you need them?"

"Stuck-up? Look who's calling who Stuck-up! There's many a man in this town hates his job, but they love their families enough that they stick to the job, regardless. Regardless." Lizzie was breathing hard now. "And bring home a regular paycheck. Regardless."

Irene rolled back on the pillows and Lizzie tenderly adjusted her bedding. Thomas laid a cool hand on Irene's hot one and patted it. "I'll be back in ten minutes."

"Where ya going?" Lizzie demanded.

"I'm getting Doc," he said, and went downstairs and out of the house.

A thrill of worry shot through Lizzie as she heard the door slam behind him. "Oh God! she's really sick or he wouldn't have gone after no doctor."

11. For over a week Irene lay upstairs and half-listened, half-lived. Commotion. Was it always like this, or just because she was sick? Up and down, mostly her mother, up and down. Noise. Eggbeaters and nagging her to eat, and neighbors knocking at doors. Suppertime, rattle silver, thump dishes, scrape chairs across floor. Smells! Delicate cinnamon, sour cabbage, hot grease—anybody watching it?—making her retch. And fights. Even the first night when Doc had come, Ma had started something. Or had Pa? "Well," Dr. Newton had said, "probably not too serious. Keep her in bed, plenty of fluids, watch elimination. Call me if she gets worse. Rest; above all, let her rest." He left.

"You knew that before Doc came," Thomas said.

"You're sorry you called him?" Lizzie stiffened to battle-ready.

"You asked for him; I just got him."

"To shut me up? How'd I know if it's something bad?"

"Didn't. 'Call me if she gets worse.' You'd have done that anyhow. He doesn't know anymore what ails her than you do. That's why it's called the practice of medicine. He's practicing."

"Considering he ain't likely to get paid, I wouldn't get too smart-alecky." She swept out of the room.

"Sorry for the fuss, girl," he told Irene.

" 'Sall right," Irene said and shut her eyes. If those two ever agreed on anything! She half-dozed and saw or imagined Lizzie's eye framed in black, looking down on a naughty boy in the front row who had mischievous blue eyes and a sandy moustache. She woke with a scream when the picture fell from its nail and hit the boy.

"What's the matter?" Lizzie shouted from the foot of the stairs.

"Just a nightmare, she's going back to sleep," Thomas answered. Irene shut her eyes and lay quiet, hoping they'd keep quiet. Maybe if she died, they'd stop. Maybe not. Too bad she'd never fit in that darling little white casket in Koelsch's window; she'd lived too long. Aah, what's the difference? Those two'd probably sprinkle her grave with tears and holy water, and be scrapping in the back seat before the limousine got to the fancy iron gate. Or maybe they'd really stop. Either way, she was too sick to care much.

Just once, Lizzie caught herself wondering if she had anything black and suitable, just in case . . . ? But she checked the thought, signed herself with a cross, and resumed her battle for her God, her children, and germlessness. Deep feelings moved her to oratory, then she remembered the sick one upstairs might be sleeping, and so her scoldings were delivered with such restraint that she developed laryngitis before the end of the week.

"Ann says you kept her at the shop picking the half-size off some shirts. Now they're fifteens, 'stead of fifteens-and-a-half. Don't tell me why, I'd just as soon not know I married a crook." The quarrel lasted a half hour, whispers and gargles of rage.

Another time, another subject: Dishes done, Lizzie was pouring scalding water over the wooden drainboard. Thomas waited, glass in hand, to get a drink. "You wait 'til I'm done," she said and aimed the kettle above the lead waste pipe.

"Oh, take your time; kill 'em all," he said.

"You can laugh. We didn't get flu all winter." He agreed. She glared. "Laugh at me and thank God. Who scalded all those germs?"

"Lizzie, I wasn't laughing. Or if I did, I didn't mean to hurt your feelings." Repentant, he patted the plump hand that was setting the teakettle back on the stove. He could be awful nice sometimes. She sighed deeply and drew away. In the battle against him, she never won. For if she did make him ashamed of what he had (or had not) done, he would try to make it up to her. Not in any suitable, sensible way that would bring a little more comfort into their lives; no, that wasn't the way of her man. He would follow her upstairs and into the bedroom and want to make it up to her. She shoved the kettle to the back of the stove. You can't win.

A week after his first call, Dr. Newton dropped in. "In the neighborhood, thought I'd just check." Lizzie and Irene were alone in the house and the doctor peeled off his overcoat and sat at the foot of Irene's bed to visit them. "How are things at school, Irene?"

"OK."

"Got teachers you like this year?"

"Most."

"Anybody bothering you?"

"Not especially."

"You always get good grades in conduct, I bet."

"She better," Lizzie interjected. "I don't care who fails in what, but they'll get it from me if they don't get Good in conduct."

The doctor shrugged into his overcoat and Lizzie escorted him downstairs. Before he left he told her, "Irene's got a nervous stomach. Keeps things to herself and worries more than average, I imagine. You want to try the light touch on her, Lizzie. Don't exaggerate things in front of her. Get a little more laughing into her life. Let her up now anytime she feels up to it, but don't rush her. Keep her home rest of this week. She's coming along fine. Good-bye."

Three times that day, Lizzie stopped her housework to amuse Irene. Once she sat on the edge of the bed and played tic-tac-toe with her. Another time she came upstairs lugging the heavy *Lives of the Saints*, thinking to amuse Irene by reading the story of St. Lawrence and how he was martyred. She read well, and she finished with dramatic flourish: "And St. Lawrence said to his tormentors, 'Turn me over, sirs, this side is quite done.' Well, I gotta quit this fooling around now and get Pa's shirts ironed. They'll be mildew if I wait for Mary." Another time she visited with Irene, telling her about Iowa. "Spring comes sooner and summer lasts longer. We ate sweet corn a month before we get it here and the woods were loaded with nut trees."

"Tell me about your dates, Ma. Where did you meet fellows if you lived all the time on a farm?"

"My mother died when I was only your age, Irene. I went to live with your Aunt Lil and Uncle Ed. Your Aunt Marie and Uncle Leo lived down the road apiece."

"Funny, my two aunts marrying two brothers. What if you had married their brother, Ma. Wouldn't that be funny!"

Irene saw Ma stiffen her back and watched her eyes go wide for a moment. Ma looked like Ann did the time she fell on gravel and it had to be dug out of her knee.

"Would it? Think I couldn't get anybody but Pa?"

"Did their brother Cletus ever propose to you, Ma, did he?" Irene's eyes shone with interest.

"You're supposed to rest, not get all worked up," she snapped. She caught her breath and said, "This doesn't get supper on the table." Water over the dam, she told herself; and "She didn't have to bite my head off," Irene was muttering.

When Irene announced the next day that she couldn't, wouldn't stay in bed another moment, Lizzie coaxed her to remain upstairs. "I got a surprise arranged for you." Then she had Thomas bring up an armchair into which Irene was ensconced while she listened to the Victrola kept in John's former bedroom. "Anytime he asks for it, it goes to him. He bought practically all the records, 'sno more than right he should have it for his own house." Irene, soothed by *Poet and Peasant*, Side I, didn't worry; the Victrola was so cowy, John'd probably buy a new phonograph with a cabinet beneath to hold records.

"Tomorrow starts a new month, you're coming down for breakfast," Lizzie promised her. "The girls'll get up ten minutes earlier so we can have a nice one." After Irene was back in bed, Lizzie spent some time cutting four-inch circles out of white flannel scraps. She carried them to the kitchen and put a batch of pancakes to rise before getting upstairs to her night prayers.

Mary and Grace wanted to make a chair with their hands and carry Irene downstairs the next morning. "I'd die if you stumbled," she said. So with Ann leading the way, they escorted her, one on each side, down the staircase. "How big and bright it all looks!" Irene observed when they led her into the kitchen. A new oilcloth was spread over the table and a little bouquet of strawflowers lay at her place. Her mother was dipping out spoonfuls of pancake batter and turned momentarily from the stove.

"Say grace while I get this batch going," she ordered. "Start in on the applesauce. Pour me some," she said to Grace, who was handling the coffeepot. "I'll be right there." A big grin spread on her face and she turned back to her cooking. She took extra care with the last four pancakes she made, adjusted the burners on the stove, and sat down. The platter of pancakes began to make the rounds. Grace was almost last to be served and she took only one, meaning to pass the platter to her father. "No, Grace, take more. The last four on the stove are for your Pa," Lizzie said, smiling broadly. She passed around the syrup, then flipped over the pancakes on the stove. She reached over the table and took Thomas' plate, then piled the four golden-brown, fragrant cakes upon it. "Just for you," she said, and handed him the plate.

He poured a stream of syrup over his cakes, lifting the top two and flooding the third and fourth. He sniffed and smiled approbation. "Nothing your mother makes better than pancakes," he told the girls. "And I'm starving." He sighed with satisfaction, then plunged his fork downward. Oddly enough, it did not sink far; it barely pierced the top cake. He grabbed his fork more firmly and began to saw with his knife. Lizzie's eyes sparkled and she had to pinch her lips to keep from laughing aloud. Thomas sawed and sawed, but no wedge of pancake resulted. The girls stopped eating to watch him and wonder at their mother's mirth so early in the morning. "Holy smoke! 'Scuse me," Thomas said suddenly and pushed his chair away from the table.

"Where ya going? Ain't you gonna eat your nice pancakes?" Lizzie asked.

"Can't. I just remembered—I left the gas burning in the tailoring iron last night. I've got to get to the shop." He shot into the front hall, grabbed his hat and coat, and was gone.

"Should I? Shame to waste 'em," Ann said, and Lizzie handed her the plate. When Ann tried to cut them, a pancake crumbled and there lay a soggy circle of flannel.

"April fool!" Lizzie laughed until her belly shook.

"I don't get it," Ann said.

"Ma dipped flannel into the batter when she made up Pa's cakes," Mary explained between spasms of laughter.

"Ma, you didn't!" Ann was appalled. Her mother was always preaching about not wasting. "Mine were OK."

"Everybody's were; just Pa's were doctored."

"Why?"

"April fool!" Ma repeated with a fresh burst of laughter. Then Grace began to laugh.

"The joke turned on you, though, Ma. Pa ran off and never knew."

"The heck he didn't," Mary said. "Want to bet that his pressing iron is ice cold? He wasn't going to let Ma get the best of him."

"Ma sure fooled him."

"But he didn't bite."

Irene listened to the banter and her heart began to sing. Ma and Pa being playful like young people almost. Old cold blowy March over, and the sun pouring into the kitchen, warming her back, lighting the syrup pitcher so it looked like glass in a church window. Wasn't it wonderful to be alive? Such a nice breakfast! Only, poor Pa. Was he hungry? Golly, that's the first time in ages that Ma and Pa laughed together and Ma laughed the most. She chewed thoughtfully.

12. Lizzie was hanging up the last basket of wash when Mrs. Affeldt came out with her first basket of whites. "That means it's close to half past eight. I should be all done before now," Lizzie mumbled to herself. "Two less to wash for. I must be slowing down. John gone now a couple of years and Matt married since last summer. And it seems like my work takes me longer than ever."

"You beat me again," Mrs. Affeldt called out. She had given up trying to be first out in the backyard after a whole summer of unsuccessful attempts to beat her new neighbor eleven years ago. But she was no sorehead. Now she greeted the uncontested laundry queen with a wave of a clothespin. "Hi! Got your dark stuff out already? My, your mister's shirts look dry already."

"They are," Lizzie agreed.

"I hear your John's going to Chicago. It's a big place. I'll bet you're worried plenty."

"Why?" He's married, he's off my hands. And they're giving him a big raise. His wife says she doesn't care where they live, if they get ahead. Now if it was my Mary, I'd be worried sick. A girl belongs home. Men can look after theirselves. Let his wife worry, not me."

"You shouldn't. You've got boys to be proud of. They're intelligent, take after their father."

Lizzie jammed a clothespin down hard onto the stocking she was hanging. "They also know how to work— they got plenty of the Pierot side of the family in them."

Mrs. Affeldt changed the subject. If talking about her boys made Lizzie so tart, maybe they should stick to her girls. "My Alice says that Irene goes out with Peter Hartwell. That's a nice family if I ever knew one." Mrs. Affeldt proceeded with the caution of a surgeon probing for a bullet. One time last year she said the wrong thing and it was two months before Lizzie spoke to her friendly-like again.

"Peter's OK, I guess," Lizzie said with no enthusiasm, "but I hope nothing comes of it." She glanced into her clothes basket to make sure it was empty, then walked over to the fence. "I'd hate to see them get serious. Irene's too young. Just graduated, just getting started working in Dr. Newton's office. I'd like to see her earn something."

"Oh, but Peter's been working for two years now and the men like him, even if his dad does own the factory. She could do worse."

"Let's not talk about it. She could have it real nice, living at home and making a steady income for years yet. Not like when I was a girl," said Lizzie.

"Ah, you just don't want to let your girls out of the nest, do you Lizzie?"

"You can say that again." She strode over to her basket and carried it into the house. "Marriage is for pigs and men," she muttered. "I'll keep my girls out of it—'slong as I can," she added. She went into the basement and pulled out the plug (they had stationary tubs now) then rolled the washing machine over the floor drainpipe. Her morning had started gloriously with herself full of pep and the August sky full of sunshine. A beautiful washday. And now that darned Mrs. Affeldt had to bring up Peter Hartwell and Irene dating. She began to hum and gradually her tune took words.

"Oh these berries! How they glisten!
Little girl, come here and listen:
Shining things will oft deceive. . ."

Why did Peter with his brunette good looks have to mess in her washday anyway?

"For the joy they give is brief—
Pois'nous berries glow in brighter tints,
Teach you to mistrust what glints."

Well, let's be thankful for one thing. My Irene won't marry as ignorant of men as her mother had been. Working for a doctor, she'll learn about things. Once she knows, she won't be in such a hurry. It's a man's world, Lizzie told her cellar walls; she'll figure it out.

Lest Irene should prove deaf, dumb, and blind to the case for single blessedness, Lizzie mapped out a campaign—not of harassment, her intentions were good— of protection. That was it. She would protect Irene against her maidenly optimism. In short, she'd keep her single.

First strategy was to urge Peter to come over as often as he liked. Keep an eye on him. It ain't a romantic place, he'll get sick of it soon enough. But Peter didn't. Apparently he couldn't get enough of the Bohemian touches: the trumpet on the Victrola, the tin lithographs covering the unused chimney holes in every room, the kitchen clock advertising a defunct insurance company. He practically lives here, Lizzie complained, and tried a new tack.

"He ain't good enough for you," was her argument, and remembered too late that Irene had been a winning debater in school. In fact, that phase of her campaign ended with Lizzie convinced that her daughter couldn't do better than choose Peter eventually. "But not now, so quit dating so much or you'll end up engaged."

"So what's so bad about that?"

"Nothing, if you could . . ." She stopped. No, you couldn't. Engagements were sacred promises and you couldn't break 'em without sufficient cause. But wouldn't it be nice if Irene did wear a ring for awhile, then . . . No, she couldn't. She'd end up with a husband.

"So what if I'm engaged. That's bad?"

"I don't believe in long engagements and you're too young."

"That's what you tell Mary and Grace, too. Anyhow, who's marrying? Who's engaged? Do we have to go through this everytime I stick my head in the door?" and Irene would leave for work, or the library, or anywhere away from the nagging voice.

Every night, Lizzie knelt and prayed as if everything depended on God. But at daylight when everything got real again, she faced the fact that everything depended on herself. She had never heard of occupational therapy, but she often said, "If it wasn't for my housework, I'd bust." Four girls interested in boys, and she could use some help with that Irene, the stubborn one. But don't expect any from Thomas; he's just as bad. Got to be his own boss. She poured a few drops of turpentine into the damp cheesecloth in her hand, them wrung it until she felt it tear. She attacked the wood and leather on Thomas' favorite chair, then approached the radio and glared at it. Full of static and you had to keep jumping to tune it in better and it wasn't worth it. Junk, all junk. *All alone, I'm so all alone, There is no one else but you.* What kind of rubbish was that to fill kids' ears with? She snapped the dial to Off and began to hum at her work. "I need Thee, Heart of Jesus, I need a Fre-eh-end like Thee."

All that summer she seemed busier than ever. She confided to Mrs. Henning, "Getting 'em out of diapers was the easy part of it. Now they eat fancier. Laundry's fussier. And you got to worry about their friends, too, what kind they're dragging home."

"You sure got a lot of company, even with the boys gone," Mrs. Henning said.

"Got to. Only way you know who the girls are with."

"Birds of a feather flock together."

"And you got to feed the whole flock," Lizzie said. "This winter we're going to be lucky far as feeding goes.

Canned hundreds of quarts. Jars all around the cellar floor."

"Fruit cellar all full?"

"Never had one," Lizzie said. "You ladies don't know what I put up with. My man ain't like some. He's no darned good around the house. I can nag him forever before he gets around to doing for the house."

Mrs. Henning suggested that maybe he just didn't have the knack.

"Nobody can be that dumb. He just don't want to learn."

"Not to change the subject, Lizzie. How come you got so much put up? Outside the plums from our own trees, I didn't get much canned. Things was kinda expensive."

"We were real lucky," Lizzie explained. "Ya know that foreigner that Thomas used to buy the house slippers from. I never could pronounce his name, an odd one. Why *we* hadda buy his slippers, I never could see. Thomas *gave* him the scraps he made 'em from. But that's my man—buying things when I needed worse at home."

"You were saying . . ." Mrs. Henning applied the phrase firmly, like a tourniquet.

"I'm coming to it. That foreigner, whatever his name is, he got a job on Commission Row. They let him take home all he wanted of the spotted stuff. It got so he was bringing home more than his wife could use. He offered to bring us the rest if I didn't waste it. Well, you know me, Mrs. Henning. Never wasted a thing in my life. This winter we'll eat good, no matter what else happens."

"I know you worked. I used to see Ann run out for sugar every so often evenings, and I could smell you canning, even at night." Mrs. Henning was one to give credit where credit was due.

"Now I got to get shelves made for all that stuff, and I'm getting fed up waiting. Thomas just better find the money for lumber and get started, or I'll give him what-for!"

Samples of "what-for" had many times intruded the Henning kitchen, disturbing Mrs. Henning, who always thought of Thomas, bookish, impractical, but gentlemanly and kind, as "that poor Mr. Davis." "We've got some two by fours left from our garage," she said. "And I'll bet Matt could bring out some scrap pieces from work. They just chop up the crates in the receiving room. Ask him. You could build your own fruit cellar for next to nothing."

The next time he stopped in, Matt promised to bring home enough lumber for bracing, and John left a few dollars under the sugar bowl after his next visit. "Get some kid to buy some one by tens, any usable scrap they have."

"Aren't you going to build it, Son?" Thomas turned to John.

"Can't. Not this week. This is a real busy one, getting ready to move. Lots of loose ends at work."

"You always said you'd do things except you didn't have to, not with sons around," Lizzie reminded Thomas. "Now the boys got their own wives to keep 'em busy. I'm not gonna wait around anymore. We'll have the lumber ready for you."

Thomas went off cheerfully enough. Sufficient to the day were the troubles thereof. He'd worry about how to put together shelves when the time came. Shucks, it couldn't be too involved. Kids did harder stuff than that in woodworking classes all the time. He had never taken a course in woodworking. Too dull.

A few days later, the Davis clan sat down to a hurried meal of fried potatoes and boiled wieners with no side dishes except lettuce with a simple vinegar dressing. "And there's no dessert, so don't leave room," Lizzie said. The kitchen was steamy hot and redolent with spices, pungent tomatoes and onions, sweet brown sugar, and tart boiling vinegar. "I'm making catsup. Didn't stop to fix much. Elsie Affeldt's brother brought in more tomatoes than she could use. Gave me a bushel. Won't keep. Dish up from the stove, everybody, on your own plate. I'll eat later." She continued to scald and peel tomatoes, occasionally stirring the pot of catsup thickening on the back stove burner. "I counted when I went down for jars. I've got two hundred seven jars of peaches alone."

"I know," Thomas replied. "I'll get right at those shelves soon as I've eaten."

It was a relief to escape into the cool basement. He had to call upstairs for Ann to come find the nails, and once Lizzie sent Mary down to hook up an extension light. "He'd never think of that hisself. I want him to see good so he can do it right."

Hours later when the catsup was cooling on the

kitchen table and all the colanders, kettles, and gear had been washed and stored away, the hammering below ceased. There were no further gratings of saw upon wood. All was quiet except for Thomas' footfalls and an occasional soft thump of jar going on shelf. It was then that Lizzie realized how bone-tired she was. Even so, she called down, "Let 'em sit. Tomorrow I'll put down papers and put 'em where I want 'em."

"Got almost everything stashed away," Thomas replied. As Lizzie began descending the stairs, he said, "I'm coming up now. We aren't going to change anything tonight. Why not wait 'til morning to look it over?"

For once, she was too tired to argue. She slumped against the door jamb, her hand over the light switch. As Thomas came up, she said, "Wash up quiet. I'm going to bed. Don't use the girls' towels. The pastel ones they bought theirselves. I'll have to trust you, I'm beat. I'm going up."

Thomas read the headlines and one long article in the newspaper, then folded it handily to the editorials and headed up toward the bathroom. He sat quietly catching up on today's events long after the mattress across the hall squealed against Lizzie's weight. Eventually he flushed the toilet, stripped off his shirt and soaped up. He splashed cold water over his neck and face and, eyes squeezed tightly shut, reached for a towel—not the one on the first dowel, that was a skimpy old white one. His dripping fingers sunk into a soft fluffy one and he knew without looking that it was pastel. He grabbed it and patted his smiling, rebellious face with it. Lord,

he'd hate to see his girls get as naggy as their Ma.
Not that she wasn't a wonderful mother, but he had expected a lot more softness in a wife. Ah well! At least
she'd be happy for a day or two, now she had her
canned goods shelves. He arranged the towel carefully
on the bar and snapped out the light. He crossed to
the bedroom but without any enthusiasm. He was over-
tired; a bit of Lizzie would have relaxed him. But after
canning all day, she refused to work after she'd gone to
bed. *Work*, she called it. Well, it takes all kinds and
none of 'em thinks like a man. Any of 'em would be
hard to live with sometimes. He yawned his shoulders
away from his ribs, stretched out his ten toes and let
them huddle back among themselves, wiggled his
buttocks into the bedding, and went fast asleep.

13. "I overdid yesterday. With all the work I done before I started on those tomatoes, it was just too much. There ain't a bone in me ain't aching," Lizzie told the family gathered around the breakfast table.

"When one finds a worthy woman, her value is beyond pearls. Like merchant ships, she secures her provisions from afar. She rises while it is still night, and distributes food to her household," Thomas intoned. There was a muscle somewhere behind his ear pulling and hurting down into his shoulder blade, and his right armpit was sore. He decided not to mention it, but to praise Lizzie's industry instead.

"*You* secured the provisions from Commission Row," Irene argued. "And Ma doesn't have to rise in the night to make school lunches anymore. But go on. Where's it from, Pa?"

He continued, "She enjoys the success of her dealings; at night her lamp is undimmed. Bible, book of Proverbs. I got a half-dollar for memorizing it. My mother, years ago. Many are the women of proven worth, but you have excelled them all. Charm is deceptive and beauty fleeting; the woman . . ."

Mary smiled broadly and Lizzie's cheeks pinked with pleasure. Grace listened attentively and wondered how Pa could stuff so much in his noodle. Except for Thomas' voice and the ticking of the pendulum wall clock, it was quiet in the kitchen.

Suddenly, a sharp crack as of lumber against concrete sounded from the cellar. It was followed immediately by dozens of crashing sounds and the tinkle of glass.

"God!" Mary had always been one to catch on fast.

"What was that?" Lizzie shrieked, and was at the cellar door before the noises subsided.

The tendons in the back of Thomas' hands jumped up and shone whitely against his knuckles. He poised knife and fork over his plate as if he could stop time if they would all go on eating breakfast pleasantly together. Grace and Ann shot dark looks toward their father; what he did this time they had no idea, but he sure looked guilty.

"Well, let's see what broke," Mary began to say. Nobody heard her. From the cellar came the most agonized shriek. It began as "Oh, no! Oh no!" *No* was cried out softly, then continued on an ascending note until it shattered into splinters. "You! You! You come down here and just see what you did. Come down here, you idiot! Just come down, you lazy lout!"

The refugee from woodworking class was not so idiotic that he didn't know when he was being paged. He pushed away from the table and bravely went down to the worthy woman. "Did a shelf break?" he asked on his way.

"A shelf! A shelf! I'll give you a shelf! What shelf? You idiot, you didn't make shelves. You made benches. Benches, not shelves. If I was a man I'd kill you." Lizzie's fists beat against her temples and she rocked her head back and forth. Thomas went toward her but she backed against the furnace. "Don't touch me, you clumsy ox. 'Ain't benches shelves?' I suppose you're gonna say. No, they ain't. You promised me shelves. Oh, my work—all shot!" She looked at a purple plum impaled on a splintered dill pickle jar. Alongside, peach halves were swimming in stewed tomatoes. "Oh, my God, my God. I'm tired. I'm sick and tired."

All the girls were downstairs by this time, and Mary explained, "Pa made seven benches, looks like."

Thomas nodded miserably.

"But surely you fastened them onto each other and against the wall, didn't you, Pa? Where are the uprights?" Mary asked and could see that Pa hadn't used any studding.

Anger surged through Lizzie's veins and gave her a new spurt of energy. "Him fasten anything? Do anything except the fastest, laziest way he knows how? Humph! you don't know him very well." She turned a spotchy face toward Thomas and bored into him with a coal-black look. "Hours and hours and hours. Never mind how tired, how hot. Peel, slice, blanch, chop, strain. Scald the jars, wash the rings, the lids. Steam and scorch, sticky stove and sticky table and me sweating like a horse on my varicose veins. All summer. And in one evening, with one hammer and one saw and no brain . . ." Here words failed her; she choked and went on, "I don't know a low enough word for you." Her eyes rolled from daughter to daughter, "In one evening, he can hurry through a simple chore—gotta hurry, gotta get back to his reading, gotta get done fast, fast . . ." Her words strangled in a sob and her shoulders shook.

"Mary, take your Ma upstairs. Get the shovel and washtubs from under the porch. Not if you're going to be late, though." He looked so woebegone that the girls could not help but feel sorry for him.

"Pa, they don't want me at the dime store 'til noon," Ann said. "I'll help."

"I'll stay home, too," Irene volunteered.

"No you don't. Sick people can be terrible troublesome. You keep 'em out of Doc's hair. We'll manage, Ann and I."

The shovel and washtubs arrived just then, and Grace watched while her father, overwhelmed, poked the shovel here and there among broken jars, not knowing where to start. "Pa, you go on down to work," she said. "Irene can phone Mr. Binner that I'll be down by ten or so. He won't have any dictation before then anyhow."

Thomas dreaded the trip through the kitchen. He could hear Lizzie's and Mary's voices, one droning on and on with lamentation, the other coaxing, commiserating. But he couldn't bear another moment with the mushy ruins that one hour ago had been golden and green and plum and red treasures hoarded against a

Wisconsin winter, so he mounted the stairs. He shut the door softly and headed straight for the front hall. He picked up his straw hat, then turned it round and round through his fingers as if trying to recall what he was supposed to do with it. He walked toward the kitchen door and said, "Lizzie, I'm sorry."

"Oh, shuddup." She said it with no expression, as one might say "Excuse me" when brushing a stranger in a crowd. Too tired for anger, she despaired of ever really liking him again.

Mary turned off the teakettle and poured hot water into the dishpan. She led her mother toward the sink. "You wash, Ma. I'll clear the table and dry when you're ready for me." She looked toward the table. "There's lots of toast and eggs left," she remarked, and her mother, who had never wasted a scrap of food since she began to keep house, said, "Throw 'em out, what's the use of always saving?" And more to herself than to Mary, "Yesterday food, today garbage. Ain't just the work. The sugar, I don't know how much. Vinegar, gallons. Spices ain't cheap. Pectin: how many dollars worth? All those rubber rings. I can use 'em again, if we don't slash our wrists fishing 'em outta that mess. All my jars. I don't suppose there's ten whole ones left." She washed the cups indifferently, then began on the plates, not examining their undersides or scratching with a thumbnail at invisible bits. Ya gotta die sometime, what's wrong with ptomaine? A big tear splashed into the dishwater and she sobbed, "And all that work, all for nothing. Too smart to do it like anybody else.

Ah no, shortcut. Benches, one atop the other and nothing to hold 'em from vibrating and shaking around. Topheavy, the whole mess." She sobbed quietly while Mary dried.

Let her get it out of her system, Mary thought. I don't know how, but she will. God help her. Lizzie gave a hiccup or two, then her crying subsided. As Mary went off to make beds, she heard her mother's vice lift in song:

> "I need Thee, Heart of Jesus,
> I need a Fre-eh-end like Thee;
> A friend to soothe and pity,
> A friend to comfort me."

What she needs, thought Mary, is a darned good rest. But I suppose she'd have to break an ankle before we could get her off her feet. She's worn out. If only I could get her to take a nap. But she'd have to be dead or hit over the head before she'd shut her eyes in the daytime. Poor Ma.

Inspiration hit Mary while she was straightening up towels and washcloths. Sedation, rather. Tucked behind a box of napkins was a bottle of dandelion wine. One of Thomas' immigrant customers made him an annual gift of it and Lizzie permitted it in the house for medicinal purposes, most specifically for her daughters' "month-lies." Her own menstrual cramps she bore willingly, welcoming them as the happy alternative to pregnancy. The wine was reserved for her daughters, none of whom cared enough for its flavor to regard it as anything but medicine. Now Mary brought forth the bottle and poured almost half a tumblerful. She carried it down to the kitchen. "Ma, here's a drink. You need to relax."

Lizzie whirled about to face her oldest daughter. "So now we drink away our sorrows. Since when? Your Pa never drinks. He's too proud to earn a living maybe, but I'll say this for him: He never took a drop. Where'd you get it?" In her distraction she had forgotten about the dandelion wine and thought she was looking at whiskey. "A girl drinking! Your Pa doesn't."

"Well, you say it yourself, Ma. Pa's different. He's always got to be different."

"You leave your Pa outta this," Lizzie raged. She was in no mood for extolling her husband's one virtue. "I've hadda put up with him before, this ain't the first time. I could tell you plenty."

"Later, Ma. I have to keep going." She went upstairs to put on make-up and go to the office after all. Ma will just have to work this out herself; no sense making myself a punching bag.

Lizzie was shelling hard-boiled eggs and slipping them into pickled red beet juice when Thomas reappeared. "Ain't nowhere near lunch time," she said without looking up.

"Lizzie, we got a telegram. The boy delivered it to the shop."

"Now what?" She dropped a half-peeled egg into the sink and leaned against the drainboard, braced for any shock. She had never received a telegram in her life.

"Lil sent it. Wants us to come on a visit."

"Why a telegram? Quit stalling. Who died?"

"Cletus." Thomas waited for her to say something, but as she didn't, he brought forth the telegram and unfolded it. "Cletus passed away last nightSTOP Services FridaySTOP Mark will meet you Thursday 11:00a.m. KalonaSTOP Don't disappoint Ed and Leo."

"I haven't a thing to wear."

"Lizzie, does that matter at a time like this?"

"I mean, I'm a mess. I could never get ready."

"The girls can help you. We're going. I must get back to the shop. We'll talk it over at supper. We're going." He left, but not to hurry back to the shop. He would have to start right in, dropping in on friends, to find one who'd lend him money for trainfare. He wished he'd done all his business C.O.D. Bet I don't get a loan from a charge-it customer. He was right. Irene's godfather thought her mother needed a vacation; he doubted she'd had a whole day off since Irene's baptism. He owed Thomas nothing, but lent him the money and secretly chalked it up to charity.

14. Clickety, clickety, clack! Clickety, clickety, clack! The steel wheels chattered on the rails beneath. At first Lizzie had been entranced. They sounded so rush, so busy, so competent. Now she hated the noise, loud, endless, promising so much and getting nowhere. She sat very straight on the plush green seat with its high backrest, staring at the high backrest in front of her. Nothing to see. Nothing to do. She turned her head to the right and saw only herself glimmering darkly in the window pane. Thomas to her left, he didn't count. Ah, here comes the conductor, stopping at each passenger's seat. Blue serge uniform, important looking. And gets a steady paycheck for wearing such nice clothes and having such a nice job, whatever it was. Won't ask Thomas. I took enough dirt from him, making benches instead of shelves. No good at anything but talking; he can just talk to himself 'til we get to Iowa. I ain't gonna make a scene there, but 'til then I ain't saying a word.

"He's collecting tickets," Thomas said. Gregarious

people are often unaware that they aren't being spoken to.

"Your head doesn't look the least bit comfortable," the conductor said to Lizzie when he punched their tickets. "You'll want a pillow."

Her face flushed with pleasure when an attentive porter handed the snowy little pillow to Thomas, but when he handed a quarter to the porter, her expression darkened. The nerve of him, throwing away their money like that. But she didn't say a word. Not even to scold would she talk to him. Anyhow, it was too late; the quarter was gone. The pillow at her back made it possible to reach the footrest and she settled down snugly. Thomas pointed at the window: "There's where electricity is generated over there where it's all lit up."

Didn't he know he wasn't fit to be spoken to? Or was he bluffing it out? She brought out her rosary and let a bit fall through her fingers. That'll shut him up. He took no offense but dozed off almost instantly.

Clickety, clickety, clack! Clickety, clickety, clack! said the wheels to the rails. And ". . . pray frus sinners nowenat t'hour uvur death," Lizzie said to Holy Mary. Her rosary finished, she would have liked to recite a litany. Funny things, litanies. You could say 'em all your life, but if you didn't have the prayerbook front of you, you'd get stuck. Well, too bad. She wasn't going to make herself conspicuous or holier-than-thou with a prayerbook. Conductor might notice.

She began a second rosary, choosing to meditate on the sorrowful mysteries. The Agony In The Garden, she announced to herself, Jesus Sweats Blood. Only it wasn't Jesus she saw in a garden; it was herself in her own kitchen. All that canning and cooking and sweating. "Send distractions far away . . ." The tune sang in her head and she pinched the bead between her thumb and finger.

She terminated ten Aves with a Gloria and began a fresh decade. The Scourging, that was next. And her motherly heart bled for the mother of Jesus. Imagine how Mary must have felt when she saw her Son! And He hadn't done a thing wrong; that was the injustice of it. The beads quickened through Lizzie's hands as she thought of a few men that deserved scourging. Well, not scourging, maybe, but a darned good jolt of justice. But justice was something would have to wait for eternity. Some people never got what they deserve. "He'll eat this winter, just like it never happened." Her mind had slipped out of the Garden of Gethsemane and back into her own cellar.

Jesus Is Crowned With Thorns, she announced on her twenty-first small bead, and I'm gonna concentrate. She poked a painfully sharp black thorn through the Eye of God in Sister Dolorosa's classroom and dozed off. The beads gathered themselves into a little gray puddle in her lap when her fingers fell open. Her over-tired muscles twitched and she awakened. With confusion she tucked her rosary neatly into her hands. She hoped nobody's gone through the aisle and noticed her asleep at her prayers. Now where was I? Fourth decade: Jesus Carries The Cross. "Blessed is the fruit of thy womb, Jesus," she prayed and indignation filled her. That He, the only perfect man, should be treated like a criminal! She saw cruel faces, cunning men trapping that dopey Pilate into executing Jesus. Ah well, politics! She didn't want any part of 'em. Dirty stuff; leave it to the men.

Fifth decade: Jesus Dies On The Cross. Fatigue was overtaking her but indignation had not quite died. She beheld her crucified Lord and wondered, really wondered, why He bothered. Almost two thousand years later, and how many people were really Christians? Twenty pews, eight people across, in St. Robert's, but twenty people was about all you got for weekday devotions. Mostly women, too; lots the men care. Except Thomas, the show-off!

The rosary had taken forever. Thomas awoke now as Lizzie heard commotion about her. "Change trains here," he said. She immediately stood up and began to reach for bags. "No hurry. We don't have to be first out the door."

She forgot her resolution and spoke: "Get 'em down, be ready when the train stops." She reached again but the bags were too high above her.

Thomas laughed. "Shall I boost you up or would you like to step on my knee?" When he saw that she really feared being left behind, he stood up and handed down the smallest bag. "I'll get the others soon as the train stops," he promised.

Lizzie felt like an actress in a play when the train stopped and the conductor on one side and Thomas on the other watched her come down the steps. The train depot didn't seem quite real. The yellow incandescent bulbs penetrated the smoky, dusty air, but not quite.

Varnished benches with scarred slats edged the room, and near the door was a counter so filled with candies and so ringed around with magazines that the clerk was almost invisible.

Thomas escorted her to one of the benches and invited her to set her bag down. She hung onto it. "Won't anybody steal it," he said.

She denied herself the pleasure of retorting, "You bet they won't 'cause I'm hanging on." To him she wasn't talking.

"I'll sit here and you go freshen up. Over there." Thomas pointed. She looked doubtful. "I'll stay right here with our bags. You better go." She went.

She was furious upon her return to see the bags unattended. Thomas had his back to them and was talking with the thick-set, short fellow behind the cigars and candies. She wanted to give him a good piece of her mind right there and then. Instead, she strode purposefully over to the bags and sat down. He needed punishing so she said nothing to him. Eventually, he turned around. "Ah, you're back. You can watch now, I'll go." She almost forgot herself, almost talked. She choked down the "Humph!" as Thomas left. By the time he returned, she scarcely remembered why she was piqued by him. She was entirely too tired to sustain any mood for long. And things were too unreal, way past midnight, the hours when at home she was up only because somebody was sick or it was storming out. Storming? She should get up and light the candles. Her head snapped on her neck. Must have been dozing. Thomas was fully dressed, sitting next to her, cupping her head against his shoulder.

Ages later, she found herself again in a train, its wheels making the same racket: Clickety clickety, clack. She looked out the window, saw only her reflection. Nothing had changed, they weren't getting anywhere, those wheels; all promise and no do. "Oh shut up!" she told them.

"Get some sleep, Lizzie," Thomas urged.

She had no intention of sleeping just because he told her to, but sleep she did. And Thomas looked down on her and saw the tired lines pulling at the corners of her mouth. He saw the sooty rings of fatigue below her dark lashes. Her right hand lay cupped upward and he saw the thick callus below the fingers and rimming her thumb edge. Her left hand spread palm downward on her lap. How rough the skin, how broken and stained the nails. She had never taken off her wedding ring in twenty-eight years. Tonight she also wore her engagement opal. She wore it only on special occasions; she took very good care of things.

Thomas wished, in a way, that he could take better care of things. But there were so many things, he argued with himself. Well, at least the important things —couldn't I take care of the important things? Well, what's important? he asked himself. And the old catechism answer came: God made me to know Him, to love Him, to serve Him, and thereby gain heaven. For a moment the answer quieted his self-criticism; he certainly loved God and searched for knowledge of Him. But serve? Did he serve God? But did he need to? God was Almighty, Thomas was just a man. Surely God needed nothing from one so limited. Unfortunately, a quotation popped into Thomas' head which drove out the comfort of not being needed. "I am the vine and you are the branches." It was true. From God came what strength he had, and he owed it to God to pass it on, so that all the branches might flow with the life-giving juices of the Almighty. Or, put more simply, take and give. Not just take.

Ah, said Thomas to himself, you give plenty. Don't be so self-critical. You're just overtired. And in another moment he was snoring.

15. "I was never so mixed up in my life," Lizzie was to say of her arrival in Iowa. "This man comes up, says, 'I'm Mark Kraemer. You Aunt Lizzie and Uncle Thomas?' And I should've known better, but I'm still thinking of Lil's boy like he's fifteen. And he pops us in this car, his, and drove through Kolona that I'd hardly recognize except St. Robert's steeple. And pretty soon we turn into the farmyard and I hardly know the house. Siding like brick, and a green roof."

Thomas interrupted. "They ruined the porch, took down the row of spool trimming, tore out the bannisters; the cucumber vine was gone and they'd taken down the swing where I sparked your mother."

"That's enough. I was telling." But she fell silent; she was still bemused by her trip.

She had stepped into the farmhouse and a gray-haired Lil came forward, and when they embraced, Lizzie had to remind herself that this was her sister, not her mother. For Lil was now fifty-six, older than ever Mother had been. She bustled about, ordering Mark to take things upstairs to the guest bedroom. "You can freshen up here," and showed them into Mark's old bedroom off the kitchen, now all white and gleaming with bathroom fixtures complete with running water and a hot air register. "Why everything's just like the city here," Lizzie marveled. "Sure's different."

But when later Lil took her into the cellar, a bit of the familiar greeted Lizzie. Jar upon jar of canned foods stood in gleaming rows. The same old crocks stood ready to receive their hoards of pickles and kraut. Three fruit flies swarmed busily over an upturned bushel basket. At the sight of all the beautiful canned goods, tears sprang to Lizzie's eyes. Lil was at once apologetic. "Here I stand talking and showing you around and you're dead tired. Let's get upstairs and set table. As soon as we eat, you've got to lie down and get some rest. That was a terribly long trip, but I thought you'd want to be here. Poor Cletus."

If Lil expected her sister to tell her how much she grieved over the death of Cletus, she was due for a disappointment. Cletus could keep. Lizzie felt overwhelmed by Lil's prosperity and the loss of her winter provisions. "Oh Lil," she began, "you can't imagine what I hafta endure from that Thomas." She began to tell Lil about her canning and how it came to naught. It was wonderful—she was right here and didn't have to spell it out word by word in a letter. Lil clucked with sympathy, snorted with indignation in just the right places. "He's so high and mighty, so educated, and can't even build shelves," Lizzie said.

Lil felt an ache of sympathy for the pudgy body with black crescents of fatigue under lackluster eyes. She reached for a jar of piccalilli as she said, "You poor kid, you shouldn't have married him."

Immediately a change came over Lizzie. Here was her sister, who knew nothing about it, telling her how to run her life, attacking her husband. Her eyes flashed. "Lots you know," she stormed. "He's real good to the children and he never touches a drop."

Lil looked at the jar in her hand, wondered what it was, how it got there. "Well, I just meant . . . I just . . . You're tired." She set the jar back on the shelf. "Let's get upstairs. You better get some rest."

The men were in the front parlor, the living room, visiting, and you could see that now people lived in it every day. In the kitchen, Lil began dishing up from a white porcelain stove. Lizzie went into the pantry for serving dishes and every shelf there had fancy paper with colored borders. But many of the dishes there were old familiars and Lizzie was comforted. You don't go all the way home just to see everything different. She handed Lil the oval dish with the goldy-brown maple leaf in the bottom and Lil spooned scrambled eggs into it; creamy and fluffy they were, like always.

Thomas, unasked, led them in prayer and when the meal was done, insisted he was going to help in the kitchen. Lizzie didn't have the strength to argue when he and Lil insisted she take a nap. "OK. I'll lie down for just a minute. I'm really beat." She slept for three hours.

Lil heard her coming down the stairs and hurried to draw bath water for her. "Marie and Leo are coming over for supper. Everything's ready, just to fry the potatoes when the men come in."

"Oh Lil, you shouldn't be spoiling me like this," Lizzie said. "I haven't been waited on like this since John was born."

"About time, then. Just get in that tub and soak and stretch. Then let's hear all about you. I heard all about the children; Thomas is sure proud of them."

Lizzie undressed. "You sure Ed won't be coming up to the house? I'll leave the door open a crack. We got to get in all the visiting we can."

"No, he never does when he's in the fields, not 'til supper. I'm going to set up my ironing board right by the door here." She ironed while her sister soaped and soaked, both of them yelling back and forth until, by the time their husbands came in, they knew more about each other's marriages than either spouse imagined.

Marie, when she came over with Leo, was generous with her praise of Lil and Ed. "It's a wonder those two ain't exhausted. I never wrote much about Cletus to you, Lizzie, didn't want to worry you. Anyhow, by the time a letter gets to you, the news is changed, makes you a liar. Besides, I figured it was up to Lil to say how Cletus was failing, seeing as how she took care of him, her and Ed."

"Cletus was never one to complain. I didn't like to write much," Lil said. "Anyhow, what to say? Strokes aren't all the same, some get over 'em pretty good, some don't."

"Lil was darned good with Cletus. Soon's he took sick, we brought him over here and she waited on him hand and foot this last time until . . . ." Ed's voice trembled.

"The Lord wanted him back," said Thomas. And hoped he'd died without telling anybody that he'd lent me money. Thomas sucked his moustache edge. Shame on me, that's a self-centered thought. Well, at least Cletus didn't need money in heaven, so it didn't really matter that he never got paid back, did it? Eternal rest grant unto him and let perpetual light shine upon him.

"You've got nothing to regret." But Leo was saying it to Ed. To Thomas and Lizzie, "You know how it was at first, Cletus farming the homestead and Ed farming his own. Always helping each other out and it got so they hardly knew whose was whose. Ed often repaired or paid for parts on Cletus' machines."

Ed interrupted. "Cletus gave me Sammy when Blackie went bad. Didn't have to. Always generous. And when our kids grew up and were helping, Cletus felt he wasn't giving as much as he was taking; he thought of it, not me: turned over all his machinery to me and we farmed both places together."

"Was his tractor new then?"

"What difference? Anything he had, he wanted us to have. Always hoped we'd land on easy street. Said a bachelor could live on less; never asked for raises."

Leo said, "No, but he never had to worry about salary cuts and lay-offs either. You were both good to him."

"Let's get on over there. The vigil's at seven."

Lizzie stood up and began to clear the plates. "Leave 'em," Lil directed. "Wilkins are coming over to do it. We better start."

"Let's go in two cars, should we? Thomas, you go with Lil and Ed; we'll take Lizzie."

"I'll sit in back," Marie said, and gave Lizzie a boost as she mounted the running board. "We got to get caught up." Twenty years of round robins and she's never come out with it: Did she ever wish she was married to Cletus instead of Thomas? To prime the pumps, Marie asked, "What did you think when you got the telegram?"

"My heart just about stopped beating," Lizzie answered. "I knew right away somebody died. All I could think was, God, don't let it be Lil. Or you," she added. Marie, an avid *True Confessions* reader, was disappointed. Us Pierots weren't the only girls in Iowa; why had Cletus stayed a bachelor? Instead of telling, Lizzie was going on about buying a dress for the funeral. "They make 'em cheap, six stitches to the inch, so Irene went over every seam; she's handy that way." Marie said nothing, so Lizzie continued, "Real smart she is, but I do worry about her."

"She's the smallest, you always wrote. Ain't she well?"

"She's wiry. I don't worry about that. But stubborn. Going with a boy and I can't break it up. She's got a good job, why should she throw it away?" Lizzie sighed with exasperation.

Here was an opening; let's get back to the subject. "Maybe she's in love, weren't you once?" Marie mentally licked her finger and turned the page.

Nosey. Lizzie didn't say it aloud but instead, "Are we coming into town already? My, Leo, this car sure rides smooth." They drove past St. Robert's where John, Matt, Mary, and Grace had been baptized. Had it been such an old church then? Hiller & Sons in the next block had their whole front in plate glass now, and gold lettering: Hiller's Sons—Realtors. She couldn't find Thomas' old shop. Mike Glancey was dead and his horse stables long gone, but none of her sisters' letters had prepared her for so much oldness and newness and strangeness.

Leo stopped the car before a large residence with a neat sign on its lawn: Harmeyer's Funeral Home. "Remember the Harmeyers, Lizzie?"

"Sure. Gracie was my flower girl." She wondered if it was Gracie's brother with the snotty nose or his red-headed cousin who was running the funeral parlor. Things sure were different. Her folks had been laid out at home. She stepped into the dim foyer where a stranger pointed to an open archway. A large sofa and several upholstered chairs took up three sides of the room which they entered. It was softly lighted and smelled of roses and carnations, sorta too rich, Lizzie thought, as she wrinkled up her nose. An alcove in the fourth wall was banked with huge ferns and against them stood the casket. A blessed candle burned on a table and Lizzie fastened her eyes on the memorial cards lying there. Thomas offered his arm and Lil propelled her forward.

"Doesn't he look peaceful?" Lil whispered.

Lizzie forced her gaze downward and saw before her a middle-aged stranger lying stiff in death. She looked curiously at the face. It was a pale mask that bore no resemblance to a young wind-burned farmer that Lizzie had known when she was younger. Here lay a man who had been sick and who would never suffer in the body again. No smarting feet, no aching legs, no crick in the back. No heartache over kids. No kids. A bachelor. Did he ever ask anybody but me? Wasn't he terribly disappointed not to get me? Poor Cletus. But God's ways are not our ways. You didn't *ask*. Thomas did, and I asked Father Schwartz. God's will be done.

What if we had married? Lizzie speculated. Would we have stayed on the farm? Would we be rich now? Would we have six kids? The still form in the casket gave no answers. She saw herself surrounded by the six kids and all of them in tears because their father had died in his forty-ninth year of a stroke. She cried softly with and for the children. Suddenly a sob broke from her. She a widow! How was she going to manage now? Six children and no father.

Thomas, offering her a handkerchief, brought her back to reality. She dabbed her eyes, realized how provident the good God is. Obedience on her part twenty-eight years ago, and now the reward: She was spared widowhood. Her breath eased out in a long-drawn shudder and she was unaware that she spoke. "Oh, God!" she said.

It was a thanksgiving prayer, but Thomas had no way of knowing. He saw her serious face, her eyes welling with tears, and heard the "Oh, God!" He thought it was reproach spoken out of the depths of unhappiness. Standing there before death, he questioned his values.

149

Had he rescued Lizzie from a hard life with a farmer? Roses squeezed together in a heart shape lay inside the coffin lid. "Dear Uncle," they said. Had he cheated Cletus of the joy of fatherhood? Had he stolen Cletus' sweetheart? Lil had said as much once when he announced his move to Wisconsin, although Lizzie had never suggested such a thing. Still, it could be . . . I don't believe it, he said. Nobody'd want that mousey farm boy if she could get an educated young man. Still, Lizzie herself was just an uneducated farm kid and maybe . . .

He looked down and patted Lizzie's work-worn hand. He thought of the canning and preserving which had cut and stained those hands, the countless apples pared, the hundreds of peaches dissected. He heard again the grinder handle going round and round, and the pickle juices dripping split splat into the basin below. He saw the jelly bag, dark with old raspberry and grape stains, and Lizzie squeezing the hot mass to extract clear juices that she cooked into jewels to spread on his bread. He placed his arm across her shoulders, so stooped from long winter nights over the sewing machine, the ironing board. His own shoulders sagged as truth hit him a blow: He really hadn't rescued Lizzie from anything, had he? Determination flared up within him and he chewed the edge of his moustache. He straightened up, quit his nibbling to clench his teeth, and swore softly to himself. Damnation, he'd make it up to her. After this funeral, they'd go back to Wisconsin and he'd get a job. He'd swallow his pride, he'd work wherever they'd take him on, he'd give Lizzie what she always wanted—a steady man, a steady income.

"Come, Lizzie, let's go sit," he said. His tremendous resolution had quite worn him out.

She took his arm and steered him to the farthest sofa. "Let's not crowd the mourners," she said.

16. Cletus lay buried and dozens of anecdotes had been resurrected, and now it was time to get back to Allistown. "I wish the train'd go faster," said Lizzie, then on second thought, "No, I don't; just so we get home safely." Thomas was pleased that now she talked to him, but he wasn't surprised; no doubt she meant to be kinder to the living, having seen death. He was almost right about it; she was talking to him out of sheer gratitude: he'd done a lot of wrong things, but at least he hadn't died. Besides, she was worrying and that needs an audience. "Ya suppose everything's all right? Darned near a week now."

"They aren't children."

"But they're at the dangerous age."

"When aren't they, according to you? Lord, how you worried that year the neighborhood had scarlet fever. But they didn't catch it."

"Didn't worry for nothing, though. Three of 'em came down with diphtheria that year."

"You worry about the wrong things, Lizzie. Stewed about Mary might get engaged to young Affeldt. And all the while it was John and Matt planning their nuptials." It still puzzled him, the little fuss she made over the boys' dating, saving the histrionics for her daughters. "You think she's taking up with him while your back is turned?"

"No, she's all over that." Lizzie looked smug. "Anyhow, he's gonna marry Anderson's Eunice. How close are we?"

"One hundred fifty still to go. Can't you just relax and enjoy not having anything to do for awhile?"

"For a woman, it doesn't work that way. I'll have twice as much to do when I do get started again."

"Will it get done better if you worry while it's waiting for you?"

No answer. Lizzie pursed her lips and began to straighten the row of buttons marching down her lap and over her knees. "You wouldn't understand, being a man. I hope it's cooler when we get home."

I could really change the subject, Thomas thought, and tell you that I'm going to get a job soon as we get home. Should I wait until I do? Will you spoil the rest of this trip with "Why-didn't-you-listen-to-me-years-ago"? But if I told you now, you'd have something to look forward to. He watched her regimenting her buttons and decided against speaking just now. It might generate too much enthusiasm. Thing to do now, he told himself, is to arrange for keeping the shop open. Won't be half so bad being in another's employ if I remain a shopkeeper myself. He thought of Capitalism, and Free Enterprise, and America the Land of Opportunity, and saw flags waving in the background. When he thought of blue-collar workers and lunch buckets, he thought of peons and peasants and illiterates and thanked God he wasn't one of them. Yet.

But no more! Lizzie had suffered enough from his high-flown ambitions. He would make reparation. He, Thomas Davis, would carry a lunch bucket and a badge with a number on it pinned to his chest. And he'd ask Dan Foster to clerk at Thomas Davis Furnishings. Dan was neat and bright. Yes, an ideal set-up: Lizzie would get a regular income and he could teach a deserving young man all about retailing; after all, he'd been in the game for thirty years now. He wished the train would go a little faster. Drat it! It was holding up both Labor and Management. A soft pull on his coat sleeve roused him. Lizzie leaned forward to get his attention.

"She won't go out after she promised, would she?"

"Who?"

"Irene."

"Not if she promised. So that's who you're worrying about. Why Irene? Seems to me you nag her more than Mary, Grace, and Ann put together." *Nag* was an unfortunate word to have used. He realized it when she drew herself tight against the window sill and turned as far away from him as she could get.

"Nag?" she said. "I'm only trying to keep her sweet and clean, is all. Thanks a lot. I don't want any Peter Hartwells hanging around all hours when we aren't home."

"Or when we are home. Woman, if you'd only realize it: they aren't children. We can't boss our girls around forever." He reached out to Lizzie and tried to turn her face toward him. His voice gentled as he said, "Lizzie, you can't keep *her* single, she won't give in easy as Mary. She's different."

"You're telling me." Her voice was edged with sarcasm. She counted on her fingers the ways in which Irene was different. One. She set her thumb down on the window sill. Irene was nosey. Wanted to see how things worked. Couldn't be scared by vague threats, and you can't spill everything, warning her against marriage. Two. Down went the index finger. She ain't modest or she wouldn't enjoy working for a doctor as much as she did. "The human body is fascinating." Was that a decent thing for a young girl to say? She probably sneaks a look in Doc's big fat books, too. Three. Down thumped the middle finger. She won't make sense. Thinks everything's got to turn out OK eventually. Won't worry. As bad as her Pa. She gave up counting and made a fist which struck with futility against the window sill. How could any mother do anything if her daughter was a bull-head? Like her Pa in too many ways. Now with Mary it was different. She'd listen to a person. And there wasn't any fight in Grace, she'd never given her mother a bad time. As for Ann—here Lizzie's eyes softened—Ann was just a baby. Things were nice now, two girls to a bedroom, no crowding. Irene better watch it, or she'll spoil it for herself. Let boys marry if they want, it's no life for a woman. She turned finally toward Thomas. "When we get home, there's gonna be some new rules."

"Good, fine," said Thomas. For he had been thinking while Lizzie had her back turned to him: When I begin to bring home a steady paycheck, I'll be head of the house, really head. And my woman will pay some attention to what I say. And if any chick of ours wants to leave the nest, we'll let her. I'll let her.

Hours and hours later, Lizzie stepped down from the train and ran forward to greet her daughters. All four had come down to the station. Thomas with his long stride was first to clasp one of them in his arms. "Irene! How did things go? Miss us?"

"Oh girls, you don't know how wonderful it feels to get off that train. What happened while I was gone?" She didn't wait for a reply. They were all here, safe and accounted for. Details could wait. "I'm dead. I'm gonna sleep like I never slept before when I get to bed tonight."

She had never been so wrong in her life, for that night she slept hardly a wink. She went upstairs early and began to undress when she heard Thomas drawing bath water. She drew a deep sigh and put her house slippers back on. Fine time to get in the tub, she thought, so close to Saturday. Couldn't he wait? But she didn't dare say too much. If she did, one of the girls would offer to clean up after him and it wouldn't do. She wasn't having any of his dirt mixing in his daughters' clothing or soiling their hands. All she could do was wait, then clean up after him. He rinsed his own tub, but that didn't get out the germs. You couldn't trust him that way. She sighed and got out her rosary. Well, there was always plenty to pray for.

She finished her last Amen and was struggling off her knees when Thomas came into the bedroom. She felt all the toothbrushes and felt foiled when she found only his was wet. Sometimes she suspected that he grabbed anybody's. She picked his towel off the floor and draped it to dry on "Pa's chair," the old straight-back that was enameled white and reserved for him only. Thomas had been delighted at her thoughtfulness in furnishing it; it never occurred to him that it was part of Lizzie's prophylactic plan to keep his buttocks off the tub's edge or the toilet lid. She brought out the scouring powder and rag and attacked the tub. It made her mad that she couldn't have just come up-stairs and gotten to bed without this job.

When she returned to the bedroom, she found him snoring and she climbed into bed clumsily, with no attempt at not disturbing the sleeper. His snores stopped and she demanded, "Why did you have to take a bath tonight?"

"Because, Lizzie my girl, tomorrow is a red-letter day."

"What's so special about tomorrow?"

He pushed down the sheet tucked under his chin and sat up in bed. He raised his right hand while his left spread flat as a book. His blue eyes shone brightly. She wondered if he was coming down with something. "To-morrow I'm going to get a job." He bowed his head toward her as if to say, "Now it's your turn. Speech!"

For a moment, Lizzie's voice failed her and she couldn't make a sound. Then the questions flew, mile-a-minute. "When did you decide this? Who is hiring you? What kind of work can you do? Have you got it or are you just talking?"

"Whoa, Lizzie, whoa. Tomorrow I'm going to apply for a job."

"Oh, well, that's different. You'll probably change your mind by noon. Anyhow, they don't take applications much after eleven; it looks like you ain't very ambitious if you don't ask for work earlier in the morning than that." She was sitting upright now, and swung her feet over the edge of the bed. "Where's my house slippers?"

"What you need them for?"

"Well, I certainly ain't gonna bounce and turn all night. There's no sleep in me now. Who you gonna ask first? I dunno . . . they're beginning to lay 'em off, I heard."

"Only in certain departments. Business is booming." He sounded so very sure of himself that she knew he hadn't a fact to stand on. "Mrs. Salwinski's brother was laid off," she began.

"Lizzie, you let me worry about it. I'm the one who's going to apply. I know more than one manager. Let's get some sleep," he urged and slid under the bedsheet.

"I'm going down and get a snack. Maybe it'll get me sleepy if I read awhile and eat." It didn't. She read the comics and they only awakened her to her new position. Major Hoople did not amuse her tonight. Why did Martha put up with that no-good husband? Why didn't she insist he get a job? She read Mutt and Jeff, and missed the point of their joke entirely. She began to reread, then set the paper aside. She got up to pour a cup of coffee. "I'm gonna be awake anyhow," she said. "I wonder if he'll actually get a job." Without realizing

158

it, she prayed, "Remember, O most blessed Virgin Mary, that never was it known that anyone who fled to thy protection, implored thy help, or sought thy intercession was left unaided. Inspired with this confidence, I fly unto thee . . ." She spooned sugar into her cup and stirred it around thoughtfully. I wonder who's the patron saint of job hunters? She sipped her coffee, then sucked her lips thoughtfully. Well, I know someone just as good, and she prayed to St. Jude, Helper in Desperate Cases. "Find him a job," she urged, "and don't let him be too stuck-up to take it. Amen."

For people who believe in predestination, it is easy enough to say that it was foreordained that Thomas would be employed the first of September of 1929. Lizzie, however, felt that St. Jude simply outdid himself. In spite of Thomas' age, in spite of last June's graduates, St. Jude got him a job. Lizzie knew that the June graduates had more horse sense than her Thomas, but the good saint had blinded the factory owner's eyes to that fact. Because she had faith, so much faith, how could St. Jude not listen to her desperate plea.

Actually, it happened quite simply. Thomas turned up at Sterling Manufacturing Company at the exact moment that the shipping department decided that one Alfred Schroekenthaler was again today not going to appear. "Still drunk, I bet," his foreman fumed at the plant manager, who was scanning Thomas' duly filled-out application form. The manager knew Thomas well and hadn't seriously considered hiring the gentleman. But come to think of it, drink was one thing Davis never did. He was hired on the spot.

17. "When morning gilds the skies,
My heart awakening cries,
May Jesus Christ be ever praised,
May Jesus Christ be ever
praised."

Lizzie sang rhythmically, sawing away exactly one slice of bread with each line of her song. She paired off four slices, spreading butter on the left, mustard on the right. She centered a slice of baloney on the buttered slices, covered them with the mustard-blanketed ones. Would have been nice to sleep a little later, but nobody else could cut a decent slice of homemade bread. She wrapped up the two sandwiches she had just made for Thomas' lunch, then picked up the loaf again.

"At work and at my prayer,
To Jesus I repair."

Thomas heard the singing and knew it was time to get up. He pulled off his nightshirt and put on a rough gray shirt and thick cotton work pants. The first time he had dressed so, he was amused at the bars of bright and dark that fell on his clothing. He looked out the window. "Going the wrong way, you know," he told the porch balusters that were casting the shadows. "My stripes ought to be going around, you know." Then he brightened. "Jail isn't all bad, not when they blow the whistle and let you go home nights." Even in jail, he would have been happy for a few days. New faces, new situations. But routine! He hated it, and within three weeks just starting off to work was drudgery. Lizzie's parting remarks weren't any help, either.

"Don't talk to every Tom, Dick, and Harry," she said once. "You hold 'em up and you might get fired." Did she think he was going to a tea party? Not in this outfit.

Another time, "You get much done at work? Remember you're fifty-three now; no kid. Don't go clowning around." Clowning around! She's got some mighty peculiar concept of what a factory's like. He tried to tell her, but there was only one thing she understood: A factory was where a man went every day but Sunday and brought home a paycheck every other week. It was that simple to her. He had tried once to describe the atmosphere. "There isn't much light coming in, always a haze of dust, and light from the skylights fades out before it reaches the floor."

She snickered. "Just like in church. You could pretend it was incense so thick that the light from the stained glass windows could hardly get through." Later that week she went to confession and rid herself of her guilt. "Bless me, Father, for I have sinned. I made fun of my religion," she said on Saturday. But

Monday, when she'd made her joke, she meant only to put Thomas in his place. Imagine complaining about dust or dirty windows! They were paying him, weren't they?

Indeed, five times they had paid him, but he never crowded up to Miss Finley's window. He preferred to watch the men and boys collecting their wages, making up little stories about them. "Old Fritz there, still sending a bit home each payday. Wants 'em to think America is paved with gold, even if he knows better now." Or watching young Tonkett (Tomcat, the other shipping clerks dubbed him): "Bet his paycheck is half gone by Monday; takes him 'til Tuesday to wake up after every weekend." The insolent way Tonkett stroked Miss Finley's hand, always accidentally, was quite a contrast to the adoring look Vito Turino gave her when she handed him his paycheck: like she was God dispensing favors. Thomas' amusement faded when he saw youngish men lined up who should have been behind desks and wearing executive clothing. "Fool kids that quit school during the war. When the Kaiser gave in, why didn't they finish their schooling? Now they're stuck." Employed less than three months, he already envisioned the day he would quit Sterling's employ, be off their payroll. He hadn't worked out any details: Lizzie's square, sturdy hand relieving him of his paycheck and her grunt of satisfaction came between him and his vision. But nothing is forever; drat it, it was absurd for a clothing proprietor to work like a peasant. An inhuman taskmaster, Production.

Now take today, a gorgeous one. The way he'd do it,

he'd lock up shop for an hour or two and take a tramp in Jensen's woods. Or see the Milanovitchs about their overdue account—the maples on their lawn ought to be gorgeous now. He heard Lizzie's voice below; she was on her second hymn already, this a sad one. Better hurry. He said his morning prayers while dressing, then told the Lord, "Don't let her get you down." On his way downstairs, he looked with distaste on his lunchbox waiting in the hall, ugly thing with domed cover. If there was any way to make it look less like a lunchbox; aah, with the kind of clothes I'm wearing nowadays . . .

In the kitchen Lizzie greeted him. "I've got you all dished up; you're kinda pokey," respectful enough, but anxious that he continue to be a good boy. He still drank his usual two cups of coffee, but didn't linger over the second.

From the living room window, Lizzie watched him descend the porch steps and a smile softened her face. Finally! Maybe he was amounting to something after all these years. She broke into a hymn to the Virgin Mary:

> "Oh Mother, I could weep for mirth,
> Joy fills my heart so fast.
> My soul today is heaven on earth.
> Oh, could the transport last."

She grabbed up a loose cushion on the sofa and walloped it. "I'll start in here today and get at the upstairs after noon. There'll be plenty of time." But there wasn't, it turned out.

As he hurried down the street, Thomas tried to sort

out replies to a question Lizzie had put to him at breakfast. Exactly what did he accomplish? Any answer would have left her dissatisfied, he felt sure. She was the kind of person who felt happiest at tasks that could be numbered. "I mended six pair of socks today." But let a day go by with only meals cooked, dishes done, troubled neighbors comforted, and a dozen household crises met, and she would sigh, "I don't have a thing to show for today." Reckoned that way, Thomas never had a thing to show at day's end either. He felt as unneeded as the kid who is occasionally allowed to stir the jelly. He looked up as he approached the Sterling Manufacturing Company and read their neatly lettered sign: "A tool is the extension of a man's hand." Nicely put, he used to think when he was a clothier. But he'd never imagined that one day he would enter the door below the sign and become the servant of the machine that made the tools. Now he entered the plant, put away his lunchbox and jacket, and was still defining his job as he took up his position near Affeldt and Murphy. "He also serves who stands around and waits," he told himself.

He was a hooker, the man who reaches up and steers the crane hook the last few inches of every trip. His job was to secure the hook to the next piece of metal to be lifted and to send it on its way. Or conversely, to undo the hook and free it for its next ride below the crane. Now he looked up at the heavy hook, all of fifty pounds, and beyond to Jim Dawson, the crane operator, riding in his cage. "Sort of makes Jim a giant, that hook. Must make him proud." Then he reflected that without himself to handle the hook at ground level, Jim Dawson would be a very clumsy giant indeed. It made him feel pretty good, but not for long. His thoughts rearranged themselves and he saw the thick ugly hook as an extension of Jim Dawson, and himself as an extension of the inanimate hook. His spirits sank. He signaled to Dawson, gears began to growl, and another unwieldy frame was on its way. Thomas didn't watch it go. The sameness, the everydayness, was getting him. Drat it, he'd talk to Dan Foster tonight. Give him two weeks' notice—well maybe four, the kid was conscientious, good for the clothing store—and get himself where he belonged, back in men's furnishings. He'd had no business getting into something like this, he wasn't cut out for it. "To thine own self be true . . ." he began to quote. He never heard the horn that Dawson was honking, he never got out of the way. The hook was descending and he was right under it. Jim pulled a lever and the hook lurched to the right. The heavy chain slid past his face, and startled, Thomas turned away. He never saw the blunt, gleaming steel hook which like an insatiable monster lover slammed at his organs and toppled him over. He lay on a bed of concrete, nerves screaming, hands trembling, his mouth open in agony, incapable of sound. He tried to draw up his knees, to close his legs, to do anything to make the pain smaller. It poured over him, red hot, splotchy, insistent and unendurable. He heard footsteps running and somebody calling out, "Hit his head?" and he heard the answer from someone with an exploratory hand on his leg, "Naw, it got him in the balls." Blackness rolled over him, and when the red-hot pain woke him again, his foreman and Mike Murphy had him up and suspended from their muscular shoulders. His legs hung limp as wash pants on a clothesline.

"Office sent for ambulance?" Mike inquired.

"Already? Just happened. Cripes."

"Just get me home," Thomas implored. "Home."

"Tell 'em in front office," the foreman said to the subdued onlookers. "I'll take him home; car's on the side street." With his free hand, he reached into his pants pocket and produced his car key. "Bring it right up to the side door here and make sure there's nothing on the back seat," he told young Tonkett, who was shoving into the circle of onlookers.

The car was waiting for them when they got outside. "Now how we gonna get you in?" the foreman demanded. Thomas shuffled toward the running board. "Wait a minute," and Mike Murphy very carefully opened the back door. "We don't wanta hit nothin'," he said delicately. "OK, now step in." But Thomas' bruised, insulted muscles would have nothing to do with his will. He thought he lifted a leg, but he remained rooted at the curbside. "We'll hafta give him a boost," Mike said.

The foreman sounded sarcastic. "You say where. Where you gonna touch him?"

"You go in first. Get his shoulders. I'll try to help on the legs," Mike said, and then to Thomas, "turn around." He waited for the foreman to get a good hold under Thomas' armpits, then he scooped up the useless legs and laid Thomas onto the back seat. "I'll stay back here if you want to start 'er up," he volunteered.

The foreman turned on the ignition and let out the clutch, and as the car jerked forward, pain scalded through Thomas' groins. His teeth bit into his sandy moustache and he tried to hold his screams deep inside himself. "Jesus, Jesus," he mourned.

"Go ahead and cuss; maybe you'll feel better," Mike was saying. But Thomas was beyond blasphemy; he was praying.

From the porch, Lizzie watched the car come up the street and stop before her house. She continued to shake her dustmop even when the man got out of the car and approached her. This wasn't the upstairs mop. She was extremely careful never to let bedroom filth recirculate into the mainstream of life.

"Mrs. Davis?" he asked and she waited, expecting him to say next, "Is your husband home?" Instead he said, "We've brought your husband home." He added in great haste, "He's gonna be all right," and Lizzie's arms turned to mush. The length of mop handle scratched over the bannister edge and fell into the ferns below.

"What happened? Is he cut? Is he bleeding?" She didn't wait for any replies but ran toward the car.

"He's gonna be all right," the foreman said, louder this time because he was so uncertain. "You phone your doctor and we'll get him in the house." When she saw how gray and sick Thomas looked, she backed away and ran toward the house.

"Gimme Dr. Newton's office," she bawled into the phone. In a minute Irene's competent voice sang out, "Dr. Newton's off . . ."

"Listen, Irene, your Pa's hurt. They brought him home from the Works just now. Two men. You get Doc over here right away, you hear me? Right away." She listened briefly, then broke in, "How do I know? He's hurt, that's all. You should see how he looks, positively gray." Then, remembering that the inquiring doctor's secretary was also Thomas' frightened daughter, she added, "He's gonna be OK," and her honesty impelled her to add, "if he lives." She hung up.

Somehow the men had gotten Thomas up the porch stairs and into the front hall. "Put him on the sofa in the front room," she said. "Thomas, tell me what happened."

He knew he couldn't trust his voice not to shake, so he made no reply. "Let's get right upstairs. He won't be walking good for awhile, Mrs. Davis." The two men half walked, half dragged him up the stairs. When they reached the landing, Mike Murphy said, "There now, you're almost as good as in bed. Just rest on us and catch your breath a minute."

Lizzie watched the three figures up there and it reminded her of the plaster plaque in church, the one numbered Five: Simon of Cyrene Helps Christ Carry His Cross. Not that Thomas was Christ; I didn't say that, God. But Mike's so big and brawny like the church's Simon. And come to think of it, that other man, whoever he is, does look a lot like the lean, mean Roman soldier in the Station. A vast anger welled up

168

in her and she pounded up the stairs. "If you get him
into bed, you can go," she told the Roman soldier. "I'd
like for Mr. Murphy here to stay, at least 'til Doc
gets here." She turned to the Centurion (she hadn't
consciously promoted him, it was just that he looked
mean and bossy, like a leader of men). "You'll want
to get back to work. Mustn't hold things up down at
the Works." Her eyes shot such black glitters that he
knew he was being dismissed. He eased Thomas onto
the unmade bed and felt sweet revenge when an oily
streak rubbed into the sheet under Thomas' shoe.

"You help her, I'll go," he told Mike. "Be sure Doc
phones us." Turning to Lizzie, he said, "I'm going now;
he's gonna be all right."

"He better be." She looked hot with rage. He didn't
even have the decency to argue about staying in case
he could do anything to help. "Let yourself out. I ain't
going down, just to come up again." She turned her
back on him and unlaced Thomas' left shoe while Mike
went around the bed and began to remove the right
shoe. She moved toward Thomas' head and unbuttoned
his shirt. Then she grabbed the shirt front with both
hands and began to pull it out of the coarse gray trousers. Thomas groaned.

"Ma'am, don't pull or jerk there." Mike carefully
loosened the leather belt and unbuttoned the trouser
fly.

"Where's he hurt? What happened?"

"There's this great big hook, see, on the end of a
overhead crane, and Thomas didn't see it coming and
it hit him awful hard." And so gently did he remove

Thomas' trousers that Lizzie didn't ask again, "Where's he hurt?" She knew.

Suddenly she was embarrassed and in her discomfort she blurted out, " 'Sfunny . . . the hook didn't hit you on your head. I mean, it was sticking right up there in the open . . ." What was she saying, for heaven's sake! "I mean . . ." but her meaning eluded herself and she ended up with, "You've always got to be different."

"Sorry, Lizzie." His voice wobbled and he said no more.

She slapped her hand across her mouth. God in heaven, he must really hurt; I never heard him sound like that, almost like he's crying. And Mike Murphy taking it all in. "Mr. Murphy, will you go downstairs so you can let Doc in the minute he gets here?" As soon as she heard Mike's steps on the staircase she tried to soothe Thomas. "I didn't mean I wished you'd got hit in the head. All I'm thinking is, I got used to the boys getting clobbered on their heads, I could cope. But what ya do for this?" She pointed in the general direction of his underpants, then dropped her hand against her apron. She felt indelicate, gawking at him like this. My, didn't men have homely hairy legs? She reached below his ankles for the hem of the sheet crumpled there and brought it up over him. "I'll cover you 'til Doc gets here," and she drew the sheet up to his chest. Out of sight, out of mind, she hoped. But it didn't work. Beads of sweat stood out on Thomas' head and every bead said hurt, hurt, hurt. She noticed how his knees trembled beneath the muslin. "I got an idea," she said. Grabbing the pillow from her side of the bed, she folded it lengthwise and placed it as a bolster under his knees. He gasped as it touched him, but soon he managed a smile. "It helps?" Her voice was so kind that it made her self-conscious.

"Some."

She was mopping his brow when the horrible thought struck her. She should have wrapped a good thick towel or something over that pillow first. Now it would never be fit to go under her head again. Oh nuts! A body can't be thinking of everything at a time like this. By the time it's over, I'll be able to sleep without a pillow. "I wish Doc would get here."

Presently she heard a quick ring on the doorbell and Mike Murphy was saying, "You go right upstairs, Doc. He's up there with his missus." Doc and his black bag appeared almost at once.

"Well now, let's see the damage. Something fall on you?"

"He got hit by the machinery, Doc."

"Where?"

"In the . . ." Words failed her and she dropped both hands low on her apron front.

"The crane hook got me, right in the crotch," Thomas said. "Got anything for pain, Doc? If I could only sleep awhile . . ."

"In a minute. Just let's take a look at the damage first." Dr. Newton gently lifted the sheet and drew it below Thomas' knees. "Let's get this underwear off." Lizzie went to the opposite side of the bed and assisted the doctor in removing the clothing. Thomas' face glistened with sweat afterward; Lizzie's went pale as she saw for the first time an adult penis, this one fast discoloring and shoved high by the swollen, purpling scrotum. Ugly, ugly, her mind said; but "Poor Thomas, poor Thomas," was all she said, and it came from her heart. She watched as the doctor softly but firmly probed muscles, thigh bones, and pubis. Finally he straightened up and said, "Nothing broken. We'll have to work on preventing any more swelling." He began to tell her to fetch some ice water, but when he saw how shaken Lizzie was, he offered to go downstairs himself for ice. "You go splash some cold water on your face and take a few good breaths, Lizzie. Then bring along some small towels."

When both returned, the doctor showed Lizzie how to wring out a cold compress and just where to place it. Then he opened his bag and brought out some capsules. He gave two to Thomas and set a few beside the water glass that Lizzie had placed on the dresser. "Continue the cold compresses for about twenty minutes out of every hour. At bedtime, give him two of these." He peered closely into Lizzie's black eyes and added, "You might take one yourself if you aren't settled by bedtime."

He left, taking Mike Murphy with him, and soon the house swelled with silence and snores (for Thomas slept now, hardly rousing when Lizzie changed tepid cloths for cold ones). Once she went toward the bathroom intending to fetch her favorite germicide to add to the cold water in the basin, but she forced herself to sit down again and think it over. "Will it help? Sure, it's bound to, the way it smells. But why bother. The towels won't get any dirtier against him this way than if he was just drying himself after a bath," she told herself. And didn't really believe it, but still she was not going to do anything about it; she was just too pooped to argue with herself. Another time, when she finished changing compresses, she wondered how come God let this accident happen to her Thomas. Was it maybe because he always had to show he was a man, no matter how tired his woman was nights? Now you're thinking mean, she said. But God is just. Ain't *that* mean. He has to punish sinners. Well, did Thomas sin? How? Just by using what God gave him? Well, what if he was piggish about using you-know-what? Wasn't that a sin? Yeh, a little selfish maybe, but who wasn't, now and then. *Little* selfish! Me dying on my feet and he'd wake right up no matter how quiet I snuck into bed. He was plenty selfish.

Thomas gave a little moan in his sleep and instantly she was all contrite. She wasn't saying he was piggish; maybe it just seemed that way when they were both young and the kids were babies and she was so tired. She heard the squeak, squawk of the porch swing across the street and knew that neighboring small kids were now waking from their naps. Presently the street began to fill with sounds, schoolchildren returning to their homes, and later the grown-ups coming from work. When she heard the front door open, she called down, "Ann? I'm upstairs, in my bedroom." Ann went up quietly, puzzled, and found her usually vociferous mother sitting strangely quiet, and her father in bed.

"He sick?"

"Not sick, hurt." Lizzie was anxious to avoid details so she sent Ann downstairs to "get things going down there."

Ann hurried down to the kitchen—she felt queer up there—and hadn't accomplished more than hanging away her coat when her sisters came in. "They're upstairs," she said by way of explaining the empty kitchen.

"Huh?"

"He's hurt." She mentioned it casually; as long as it wasn't Ma in bed they didn't have to worry.

"Poor Pa," Irene said. "I wanted to come home early but Doctor said Mom would manage. How's he look?" Without waiting for an answer, she sprinted upstairs followed by Mary and Grace. They felt awkward in their parents' bedroom; they had never seen Pa sick enough to be upstairs in bed in the daytime, never. Irene seemed the only one who was at ease. She held his wrist, took his pulse, and kidded him a bit. Lizzie watched with mixed emotions. She was glad if Irene had the makings of a good nurse—somebody had to do it—but wasn't it more natural to blink and talk fast like Mary, or blush like Grace, or sneak off as Ann had? Irene offered to stay with her father so that Lizzie could supervise in the kitchen. But Lizzie, who was feeling vaguely penitential, refused to go down. "Then I'll bring up a tray and you can feed Pa and yourself right up here," Irene said.

When she came to fetch the tray afterward, Irene announced that she was going out that night.

"With Peter?"

"Well, natch."

"With your Pa laying here sick?"

"We didn't know Pa'd be sick. As long as you don't want to leave his side, what difference?"

"Listen, don't get snotty. I don't want you starting anything with your Pa laying here sick, but I'm telling ya, ya better watch it. You're only nineteen."

Irene set her mouth primly and forced herself to sound amused. "You were an old lady when you dated Pa?"

"Don't get smart. It was different in those days. Everybody knew everybody. We didn't go to movies and sit in dark autos afterwards." Lizzie stopped short. No, that wasn't right. It was somebody else had an auto, not Peter. Before Irene could point that out, Lizzie plunged on. "You got a decent job. You got it good. You don't hafta run after boys." She didn't wait for rebuttal, just collided head-on with what was worrying her. "See that he keeps his hands off you."

"He's a fine boy. Have a nice time, girl." It was Thomas.

"Should I hold his hands all night so he can't?" Irene asked. Thomas smiled his amusement and Lizzie clamped down on her back teeth. That's right, encourage her; oh, men! When Irene saw that her little joke didn't amuse her mother, she thrust the food tray shoulder high and swaggered out of the room like a smart-alecky waitress. But she stopped wiggling her hips as soon as she disappeared into the upper hallway. Vexed with herself, she thought, "That was stupid of me. With Ma, dating is no joking matter. Ah well, least it takes her mind off her troubles. Wonder how long before Pa's up and at it again."

Thomas listened to her heels clicking down the stairs. "That's one we don't have to worry about."

"*I* do. She's the only one that doesn't take after my side, not at all."

"Nice for her, working for Doc." Thomas steered the conversation away from his deficient lineage. "She's bound to benefit from the association." He was thinking of Dr. Newton's college diploma, his involvement in civic affairs, his hobnobbing with professional people.

Lizzie nodded agreement which wasn't agreement at all. "Yeh, I'm sure glad she found the job." Glad was too mild a word, really. She was overjoyed at the way God had shoved Irene into a job where you had to know Those Things. All afternoon she'd had plenty time to think about it. You hafta keep your daughters pure and how can you, if you tell them things? You can't tell 'em ahead of time, 'cause then they get to thinking impure thoughts. But Irene was lucky. Sunday after graduation, right after Mass, Dr. Newton had come up to Irene and asked her to work for him. No doubt he had all sorts of books about You-Know-What and it would be her duty to read up on It. And she'd learn plenty just from patients coming in for one thing and another. Wonder how much she gets to see? Well anyhow, thank God, the way it is, I don't have to tell her nothing. If she does marry, she'll know what she's asking for. "Time for another cold towel on you,"

Lizzie said to Thomas. "I'll fix you up now, then I'm going down to try and get caught up. I sure didn't get much done today." She drew the terry cloth from the icy water, folded it on itself and gave it a mighty twist. She avoided his eyes as she drew down the bedding and placed the compress against his injured organ. Ugh, it sure looked different from anything she'd ever imagined, and such a hideous color, like blood sausage, almost.

"Easy, easy, Lizzie." Thomas implored.

"I'm not touching you, that's just the towel." She arranged it to her satisfaction, pulled up the sheet, and straightened her back. Then she looked straight into Thomas' eyes and her eyebrows winged downward.

"What's the matter, Lizzie?"

"I'm telling ya, if you get over this, you aren't going back to that Sterling. You could get killed and lots they'd care."

Thomas grasped her hand in both of his and shut his eyes for a moment of prayer. Not prayer, but jubilee, hosannas, hallelujah! Yessir, he'd picked a winner when he picked his Lizzie. Maybe she had sounded shrewish now and then, but basically she was the same sweet girl who'd fetched a pretty blue cup, drawn up a refreshing drink of tangy cold well water, and said to him, "You mustn't overdo it, Thomas." Oh God, he was a lucky man. No need to lay any strategy for removing himself from peonage. All the scheming about getting dismissed without actually getting fired . . . all the reasonable approaches and elocution that would have wilted under Lizzie's scrutiny . . . forget it! She herself was terminating his employment as a factory worker. God is good! "I think maybe I could nap now." He squeezed her hand. "You've got me feeling much better."

18. "I won't sleep a wink, but it ain't because I don't need it," Lizzie told herself as she made her nightly rounds. It was dark now and, except for Thomas' snores, dead quiet in the house. Mary and Grace were sprawled face down in their bed and Lizzie could see the lumpy curlers poking their heads. "How they can sleep with them in, I'll never know," she said, and then explained it to her own satisfaction: "Why shouldn't they sleep? What they got to worry about?" She thought of Irene, still out on her date. "They don't know what this all could lead to." She pulled a second blanket up over their knees, then crossed the hall to the Boys' Room. Irene and Ann had a kidney-shaped vanity table where John's desk used to stand on the east wall. The paint that Irene had brushed on the walls was orchid, and the boys' old brass bed was replaced by a painted wooden one with a floral-sprigged spread. Nevertheless, Lizzie still referred to the chamber as the Boys' Room, and Ann never could figure out why Irene would laugh and say things like, "Run upstairs and get my nail polish from the Boys' Room," and Ma would scowl.

Ann lay in the pretty painted bed, one arm thrown above her head, the other flung across Irene's pillow. Lizzie smiled at her baby. Such a pretty girl. She tiptoed forward and moved Ann's arm from Irene's pillow and covered it with the sheet. Irene should be coming in pretty soon and she didn't want her waking Ann.

"I wish she'd get home. Between her and her father, I ain't going to get a wink of sleep tonight." Lizzie withdrew from the room, got a fresh sheet and pillowcase from the linen closet, and headed for the staircase. She came down the first three steps rubbing her shoulder against the wall, hoping to quiet her footfalls. Then she came to the landing and reached out for the bannister gleaming softly with reflected street light. She put her weight hard into her hand as she went down the next step. Darned. It squeaked in spite of her care. But nobody upstairs stirred. She didn't want them waking and arguing with her, telling her to come to bed and get some sleep. She knew when she could and when she couldn't. Between those two, Thomas and his I.M.A., tonight was going to be a no-rest night.

Not that Irene'd do anything wrong. But it's almost eleven and she isn't in yet. She's a good girl, no doubt, but dating was the riskiest thing you could do, so many occasions of sin. She could get all worked up and warn Irene about it, but she couldn't help wondering. Did it do any good? Or did it maybe just put ideas in her head? Once when she said to her, "Don't sit tight against him, leave some room for the guardian angels," Irene had just laughed. Maybe she shouldn't have said it; maybe Irene and Peter never sat tight until she suggested it. Lizzie sat down hard on the sofa and rolled her eyes upward. Three of 'em asleep up there, why couldn't it of been four? Why doesn't Irene just settle down too? Always different.

Like her Pa. He was another one. Swaboda, Murphy, Ellis. They all worked at Sterling and they never got hurt, not that I ever heard of, and they been there for years. Then *he* starts work there and in a couple months he's hurt. Not a sprained wrist or a smashed thumb— or anything you could talk about. No, he's got to get injured in the most embarrassing . . . Words failed her and she turned to a new grievance. How long's he gonna be laid up? It was a question she couldn't answer and it turned around in her mind until it bloomed out into an enormous frightening question: Would he ever get well? She'd heard of bruises that eventually turned into cancer. There was Lorraine Sheals, for instance. Cancer of the leg bone, and Lorraine's mother remembers how her girl was hit on that very leg by a toboggan and it never healed. Couldn't have been hit so hard, the leg didn't break. But it musta been, cause it turned into cancer. And legs are harder and can stand more than . . . Oh God, please don't let his turn into cancer.

She was breathing fast and wringing her hands when she heard matched footfalls coming up the sidewalk and onto the porch. She took a deep breath and shuddered with relief. "They're home!" She reached toward the lamp, but changed her mind and sat in the dark as Peter opened the door for Irene and stepped inside. The silence was thick as wool for a minute, then Peter said goodnight. Irene softly shut the door and began to tiptoe upstairs. Lizzie turned on the light and pinned Irene to the bottom step. "I'm in here, waiting up."

Irene came toward the sofa, her hand caressing her lips, blue eyes aglow and faraway. She blinked and focused. "Oh Ma, you shouldn't. You'll be dead tomorrow."

"I could say the same for you."

"I don't get up as early as you and I haven't been nursing Pa all day. How is he?"

"Sleeping now."

"Ma, get to bed. You look beat."

"Lots you care. I can't sleep 'til you're all in and you know it."

"I'm in. Come on up."

But Lizzie refused to budge. "I can't sleep when I'm worried and I can't sleep the way he's snoring. Lemme be." She turned out the light and Irene slipped upstairs and to bed.

"Now why didn't I talk to her while I had her down here?" Lizzie asked herself. "I'm just too distracted tonight." She covered the sofa bolster with the pillowcase and spread out the sheet. "Maybe if I lay down and say my rosary, I can rest that way." She was asleep before the second decade crept through her calloused fingers.

Irene pounded on the bathroow door. "Can I come in, Ma? Have to get ready for work."

"Soon's I finish up. 'Nother minute."

There was no key or bolt on the door, yet no Davis ever opened the bathroom door without permission.

Thomas had always felt that a large family needed its moments of privacy and, while beds and living rooms had to be shared, one room was uniquely suited for being alone in. Lizzie too never allowed the little ones to congregate in there. There were other places to play, not so germy. She came out now, her hands still damp and stained a dirty brown color well past the wrists. "I was just soaking the towels in D.O.D.," she explained.

"You'll never get the stain out, Ma."

"What's the diff? Ya think I'd use 'em again after where they been?"

Irene hated D.O.D. Pretty, pretty violet-red solution until you pulled out your foot or your hand or whatever Ma had you soaking, then the air caused it to turn dirty brown. It didn't wash away, it had to wear away. Ugh. "You sure got your hands looking a sight."

"Maybe, but I *know* they're clean, cleaner than clean. You can see where D.O.D.'s been." She headed for her own bedroom, wondering if she shouldn't have put some D.O.D. in the icewater compresses yesterday. Thomas' crotch was horribly swollen and he lay with legs spread far apart. D.O.D. never hurt anything, far as she knew, and maybe it would've done a lot of good.

Irene in the bathroom squeezed toothpaste on her brush and stuck out her tongue at the pail of old towels soaking in the tub. She began to brush.

"Hey, can we come in? It's getting late." Ann spoke for all.

"Yeh, I'm only brushing."

"Spit in the toilet so I can wash up?" Mary said.

"OK," said Irene so agreeably that Mary was surprised.

"Stay to one side so I can see too," Ann told Mary. "Can't you do that in the bedroom? You've got a mirror."

"Need water," and she poked a tiny sponge under the cold water faucet, gave it a squeeze, and rubbed it over her powdered face.

"Ma didn't let me use powder in high school," Mary remarked.

"I don't let it look like I fell in the flour barrel. 'Apply sparingly, then set with cold water.'"

"It's a gyp," Grace said. She had just washed her hands under the bathtub spigot and was pushing back cuticle with a bath towel. "You use nail polish too."

"Yeh, how often?"

Irene wiped her minty smeary mouth against a damp facecloth and banged the toothbrush against the tin medicine cabinet. "Announcement! Or would you rather wrangle?" She waved her left hand around, rippling her fingers through the air, dropping them gracefully to let her whole hand dangle from the wrist. The electric light on the ceiling was reflected in a hundred sparkles from a ring on her third finger.

"Hey, he didn't!"

"Hahoo! When?"

"Irene, you can't." This like a sob almost from Mary.

"I did. Why not?"

"I'm the oldest. I ought to be married first."

Grace turned to Mary and said, "Be grateful. Good

old Irene. Always in the doghouse anyhow; let her be the trailblazer."

Irene turned the ring back and forth on her finger, watching the lights refract. "We're not getting married 'til next September. Anybody else wants to, go right ahead of me."

"First we gotta catch one," Ann said and laughed.

"Too bad you aren't the oldest. Ma lets you get away with anything, seems like. I suppose she'll just hit the ceiling when Irene tells." Grace popped a thumb into her mouth and pushed away at the cuticle with her lower front teeth.

"Hide the ring, you don't have to tell," Ann urged.

"Listen, I'd rather listen to 'em"—she referred to Lizzie Lamentations, her private name for all the arguments and protests her mother inflicted upon her— "than sneak. If I have to, I'll fight."

"Do you have to?" Mary asked.

"Tell? Certainly."

"No, marry, I mean."

"Sure I have to. I'm in love. I'm supposed to stay single just to keep peace? I'm telling her now."

She also was telling her father, but he wouldn't object; he almost always approved what she did. Thomas liked action, changes. About all she expected out of him was the old saw about not losing a daughter but gaining a son. She hoped Ma wouldn't take it out on him, not while he was sick, anyhow.

"Quit visiting, girls. I gotta get in there." Lizzie had been downstairs for ice and had arranged another cold towel on Thomas' bruise. She sat now with hands clasped together, careful not to rest them on her lap. I'll get in there and wash 'em thoroughly when those girls get out of there, if they ever do. Unconsciously she turned her hands upward, until they were in an attitude of prayer. God, please God, help Thomas. His business looks worse than it did yesterday. Oh please, don't let it turn into cancer. He never was mean, he never drank, he don't deserve it. Please.

Suddenly the doorbell rang. Three girls ran for their rooms and Mary wrapped her chenille housecoat more tightly about her. "I'll go down." When she returned, it was with Dr. Newton, who explained as he came up the stairs, "I wanted to stop before I go over to the hospital. I'm taking out an appendix this morning and it might get towards suppertime before I get the chance to see Thomas." In the upstairs hall he said loudly, "Irene always books appointments as if I were twins," and she answered cheerfully through her closed door, "Two thirds of them don't have appointments and you never let me turn anybody away."

The doctor went to the foot of Thomas' bed and noted the wide inverted Y that he made under the bedclothes. "Really tight, eh?"

"Like a drum. You wouldn't believe how it throbs."

"I think we can take away a lot of that pressure. Let's take a look." He folded back the bedding, removed the compress, said hmmh, just what I thought, covered Thomas lightly, and opened his brass-bound bag.

Lizzie peered curiously inside and noted with approval the neat row of bottles marching along one side

186

of the bag right below the opening. She recognized the stethoscope lying below and observed tongue depressors in a glass jar with a screw top. Clean, that was the word for Doc. She watched him bring out two gauze-wrapped somethings and a test tube with a wad of gauze for a stopper. He unwrapped one of the things, then the other. Glass they were. Heavens! When he fit one into the other, it was the biggest syringe she had ever seen. And now from the test tube he extracted a hollow needle, and she never exaggerated but it was bigger than any darning needle she'd ever used.

He exposed Thomas again, gently rubbed a spot with something from a colorless bottle, and said, "I'm going to aspirate. You'll feel a lot more comfortable after." Then he plunged that enormous needle into Thomas.

Lizzie felt her knees melt and slide into her shoes and there was nothing below her ribs to hold her up. She grabbed hard onto the chair back and Doc's heavy butt kept the chair and her from pitching over. She wanted to look away when the dark red came up from the needle like mercury rising in a thermometer. She wanted to shut her eyes when the red widened out an inch in the syringe. She wanted to scream when it lengthened and climbed upward behind the plunger as Doc drew it higher in the barrel.

Thomas had gasped a little when the freezing cold ball of cotton had touched him and he bit his upper lip and began to gnaw the edge of his moustache when Lizzie began to look so queer. When he saw her face go pale and saw how her hand shook on the chair back, he couldn't help her. Doctor was treating him too painfully. Well, what had to be, had to be. Nothing, nobody was going to make him yell out while his woman stood by taking it all in. He clenched his hands and sank them hard against the mattress. Did the lions in Nero's Colosseum go for a man's face or for his vitals? Lord, who would have thought that the organs that promised so much pleasure to a young man could be so damnably painful? Women, always saying it was a man's world, little they knew. Did ever a woman's sex organs hurt like this? Certainly not. Even the Bible said so. "And when a woman is about to give birth, she forgets the pain for the joy that a man child is born." But I'll remember this if I live to be ninety-nine.

The doctor was finished. He turned away and Lizzie sat down hard on the edge of the bed, her back to Thomas. Her ears roared and everything, dresser, walls, mirror, went red. She heard Irene and a man talk, who she didn't know. Somebody sort of half carried her somewhere. She awoke on Irene's bed and knew she must have fainted. They shouldn't have put her filthy shoes on the bedspread. Now that'd have to be washed. As if she didn't have enough. She came more fully awake and remembered that awful needle. Pity for Thomas swelled up in her; she never wished sickness on anyone. In her mind she saw the needle plunging into soft tissue again and again, and anger surged in and crowded out her softer feelings. It just wasn't fair. It ain't right that Thomas should get all roughed up like that. OK, so he poked me plenty, but for a machine in a factory to poke him one great big one back? And with everybody watching? She was furious; they could beg on bended knee, she'd never let him go back there. They could starve, he's going back to his own business. Least it had dignity. She saw Thomas again, legs sprawled, needle stuck straight into him. She shuddered. I never knew men could suffer on account of their sex. My Lord, they didn't have it any better than the women. Lord have mercy!

She got up from the bed and went to check on her husband. His eyes were shut and hers misted when she saw the dark circles below his. Her hand went to her mouth, she darted her eyes to left and right and saw that she was all alone, and she blew him a kiss.

"I saw that." His blue eyes popped open.

"I didn't do it," she said.

Their workday was over, but none of the Davis girls was making the dinner. Irene had promised the others that she would announce her news as soon as she got home, and they were all upstairs now.

"Ma, Pa, look what Peter gave me," she was saying.

Thomas raised up one arm and drew her closer to him. His face lit up while he examined the ring. "So, I.M.A. Davis is going to become I Was A Davis."

"Oh, Pa, I'll always be a Davis."

Lizzie was stunned, but she thought something ought to come out of her. "Mrs. Peter Hartwell." She repeated it. "Mrs. Peter Hartwell. Well, at least it's a pretty name. And you could call your first one Elizabeth Hartwell. Elizabeth Ann Hartwell. That goes real good."

"Ma," Mary said, "she ain't even married yet."

Lizzie nodded mutely. She wasn't, *yet*. And if I'm

gonna do anything about it, I ought to now. But what? And for the first time in her motherhood, she asked: And why? God created them male and female, I didn't. Sure, it's hard on a woman, but a man's got problems too. They need us; I 'spose we need them, too.

Listen to those girls chattering. Did we make that much noise, Lil and Marie and Miss Hammond and me? I'll bet not.

"Let's have 'em in pastels, each bridesmaid a different color."

"Rainbow."

"And a pot of gold at the end of the rainbow."

"Potty chair, you mean."

"Will Peter rent a tuxedo?"

"What for? Big expense for only a couple hours."

"Ain't. It's for life."

Thomas broke into the prattle. "Clothes make the man. Give the ceremony its due. Dress up. Three priests and three chasubles for one Mass, when it's a solemn high."

"I'm afraid you'll have to settle for just a tux, Pa."

"You want it formal, don't you, Irene?"

"Let her say; it's her wedding," Lizzie said.

"Gee, Ma, thanks." Irene spun her engagement ring around and around on her finger self-consciously. Finally she positioned the diamond exactly below her knuckle and blurted out, "I was afraid you'd throw a fit."

A slow blush crept up Lizzie's face and the girls retreated down to the kitchen. Thomas lay staring up at the ceiling but he found no answers there. Was Lizzie just going to let go? She who could put a hell-fire-and-damnation revivalist to shame, and did, whenever the girls came in from a date . . . He tried a bit of conversation, just an experiment: "She's done it, she's grown into womanhood. Irene Margaret Agnes Hartwell. I'm not sure I'm completely sold on the idea."

"It ain't your wedding." Lizzie sounded snappish.

"There's risks." He didn't say for whom. "Guess I know the feeling when an Inca father finds out it's his daughter they picked for the annual spring sacrifice."

She knew what he was referring to. She and the kids had been to the museum in Milwaukee and seen the huge diorama there. "You always did talk silly. No heathen's laying a finger on her. It's perfectly decent."

Thomas crossed his arms over his ribs, like he was hugging himself. His mouth shaped itself for laughter. As she watched him, the bird wings drew dangerously close over Lizzie's piercing black eyes. "Perfectly decent," she repeated.

He was all atwinkle and wanted to hear her say it again. "Marriage is? Lizzie, you're sure?"

She sniffed. Sometimes you'd think he was the one that only had a fourth grade education. She tried not to sound angry, to be patient with him. "Perfectly decent. If it wasn't, would they do it in church?"